This is a
Chair

A Lyrical Tale of Life, Death
and Other Curriculum Challenges

Craig Loomis

THIS IS A CHAIR

Published by Sixty Degrees Publishing LLC
Sixtydegreespublishing.com

Interior design by Jose Ramirez, Pedernales Publishing LLC.
Cover design by Michele Bowker and Jose Ramirez

For information about special discounts for bulk purchases, we would be happy to hear from you. Please contact us at: Michael@Sixtydegreespublishing.com.

10 9 8 7 6 5 4 3 2 1

Library of Congress Cataloging-in-Publication Data is available with publisher.

Craig Loomis, Author

Contemporary fiction – humor 2. Fiction – academic drama3. Humor – School Setting 4. Professor and his students – drama

Trade paperback ISBN: 978-1-7371846-3-8

eBook ISBN: 978-1-7371846-4-5

xx-v5

If arranged correctly, shards of smaller stories, slivers
of images, portraits of people and fragments of places
can be marbled and mixed in such a way as to create a
larger more comprehensive narrative. This final mosaic
will assume its own life.

Kama tushakel alfusayfes' alsurah

"This is a chair. Repeat."

"His ah snare."

"This is a chair. Repeat."

"This his ah hare."

 "*Lah, lah.* This is a chair. Again."

"This is a care."

"Chair, Ch… ch….ch. Chair. One more time."

"His ah Sn. . .sn . . . sn. . .snare."

"*Nam.* Very good."

1

"Her final grade was F. Or more precisely, that was the final grade she earned, the operative word here being 'earned'." He says this angled behind his desk, with one hand at the ready, in reach of his computer, the other clutching a well-gnawed yellow pencil. And almost immediately I feel exhausted.

"Ok, fine, but any idea as to why she is appealing this grade? As you suggest, what's to appeal?"

He shrugs the shrug of having to endure an unimportant question. "Actually, this was one of the easy ones: what? 48%, but no, let's be extra precise here," as he stops to squint at a paper in front of him. "47.7%, but never mind that, because I am sure she feels…what do they call it…?" holding the yellow pencil tight against his temple, "…ah yes, disrespected." Re-angling himself, he takes a deep sigh, almost as if he is getting ready to hold his breath and slip underwater. As a rule, my sighs are different, shorter, less breathy, weakly dramatic. His sighing all done, "Come on, Martin, you know how they are, it's an old story of medical woes: a cough, sore throat, extra tired, stomachache, 'didn't feel right', who knows. Of course, I don't accept any doctors' notes. Never have." As he turns to his best lecturing, matter-of-fact classroom tone. "As you well know, they can get these pieces of paper anywhere, at any clinic for five dinar, not even that, somebody knows somebody's cousin, uncle, you know how it works. Besides, when she misses that many classes, never mind the 47.7%, what's to do, to say? I can't even pretend a 'let me think about it'."

Meanwhile, the yellow pencil is now against his lips, his re-angling bringing him back to his computer screen. I think I should feel snubbed, but I don't, can't, and so, "She insists that her medical excuses were ignored, that you never even bothered to look at them, that you just tossed them back at her. Her words: 'never bothered' and 'tossed'. Please tell me this is simply student angst gone awry, John."

Dr. John Redmann is a Medievalist, who, they tell me, has written important papers on Sir Gawain and the Green Knight and The Song of Roland. I know very little of medieval times, let alone its literature. Of course there was the black plague, the hero-criminal Robin Hood, as well as assorted literary folks like Boccaccio and Chaucer. When John was first interviewed, wearing what could only be described as somebody's borrowed too-small blue suit, I remember him mentioning as an 'oh, by the way' his ancestry, something about being one-eighth Comanche—or was it one-fifth Apache? But that was some nine years ago, the one and only time I ever heard his claim to Native Americanism—Dr. John Redmann. Because John is a Medievalist, by default he abhors teaching anything that smacks of a writing class; in fact, he does not care for teaching at all; he would rather do his research, and every semester when it comes to scheduling, he reminds me of this in an official departmental memo, insisting that 'my important scholarly investigations demand my undivided attention,' and 'I simply cannot be chained to teaching what amounts to high school writing classes', etc. My response has always been, in a return departmental memo, "Yes, I understand, Dr. Redmann. Noted." He, like the rest of us, will teach his two sections of Freshman Composition.

Done staring into his computer screen, John gazes down at his hands as if suddenly there is something important there, something that requires his immediate attention, and now a token glance my direction, until "I don't remember all of that. Why should I? But if she said it, I am sure it must be true, the bits and pieces of disrespect, right?"

"John, I am not the enemy here, you know that. Nobody likes these grade appeals, and yet we all go through them, every semester, and now congratulations, it's your turn—again."

"Yes, yes, I am sure." Turning to face his computer, and now typing something that apparently cannot wait.

This means we are done.

As I leave, he ends with one final getting-ready-to-go-underwater sigh, concluding with, "And please shut the door behind you."

I take the long way back to my office, winding through the warren of cubicles, to the other side of the building, facing the Gulf. Almost everybody says that I have my desk facing the wrong way, that I need to turn it around so I am looking out over the murky bluegreen waters of the Gulf, so I can watch the oil tankers and cargo ships drift by like so many tiny towns. They may be right. When students come in, they admire my fifth-floor view, the girls keenly interested in their own reflections, rearranging their *hijabs,* turning this way and that, puckering their lips, until, finally, like somebody's waiter, I have to ask: 'How may I help you?' The boys, not so much, maybe stopping long enough to watch the pigeons strut along the window ledge, only to flutter away, to do their ticktock walk on someone else's window ledge, another perch, any telephone wire will do. How can any creature spend its entire life flapping about, hurrying from one perch to another, two minutes here, thirty seconds there, and call it the stuff of life? The more I consider it, the more I think about locking my office door, but then, at the last moment, change my mind and head towards Simon's office.

I walk down the hallway, past the Spanish adjuncts who are playing their too-loud Samba music and laughing. They tell me their classes are always some of the first to fill every semester. And every term they earn an official memo from John, complaining about their being too loud, too joyful, interfering with his lectures, disrupting his office hours, etc. I respond yet again with a 'Noted.' Stopping in front of Simon's office door, our resident art historian, it is closed, locked; I give the knob a brassy twist but nothing comes of it. I squint to read the tiny notice on his door that says yes, he has office hours now. Peeking through the smallest of slits of his hallway window, I can see him, behind his desk, feet up, shoes off, earphones on, a dreamy look on his face as he scans the ceiling. Simon's office hours: door locked, earphones on.

Hands in pockets, I head back toward my office but as I take the corner I see a student lingering at my door, hand at the door-knob, and I quickly lurch to the left, heading back towards the Samba music. Hovering in mid-hallway, I look down and notice for the first time that the carpet is a brown gravy color. I didn't know that, and stop to stare, toeing it. Without thinking about it—turkey-gravy carpet on my mind—I have come to a halt in front of Sara's office, her door yawning open, inviting.

Dr. Sara Crane is twice divorced, childless, mother to three cats; she knows all there is to know about feminism and Jane Eyre. Sara is secretly famous for taking the same Jane Eyre article ("The Man-Made Mad Women of *Jane Eyre*") and recycling it multiple times –altering the title, rearranging sentences, a new footnote here and there; at last count she has morphed it for at least five different conferences—earning university funding each and every time. I haven't decided if the right word for Sara is clever, or not. And who can forget that day after Spring Break last year, after a dust storm had kept everybody indoors for two days and two nights, when she came to campus leaning on a well-polished lacquered cane.

"What happened to you?"

"I fell."

"Ankle?"

"Ankle and knee."

"How did you do that?"

A shrug, "The regular way, nothing special, more a misstep than anything else."

I nodded, as if that were a fine answer.

"As a matter of fact, come to think of it," jabbing her cane at a dark stain on the carpet, "speaking of my health, it looks more and more likely that I will be sick next Wednesday and Thursday, if truth be told."

I watched her closely to see if that was code for something else, watching her mouth for anything like a smirk, a hint of grin.

"How do you know?"

"What?" leaning on her cane with a grimace.

"How do you know you'll be sick next week? Next week is next week."

That's when she stood just a little taller, straighter, announcing, "I know these things, believe me. A woman knows when her shenanigans are approaching."

As a rule, Sara Crane does not care for being challenged. As a professor, she is of the mind that she has earned her fair share of respect, studying long and hard to know what she knows, and so on. And so, who was I to question her shenanigans?

Because Professor Crane often has the shenanigans, Reedah is forever placing signs on her office door that read "No Classes Today." So there you have it, the good professor calling in many times every semester to claim sickness, along with assorted bouts of shenanigans; as a result, it is impossible for her to teach, to make the mandatory assessment meeting, and of course holding office hours this week is out of the question. "I tell you, my shenanigans are relentless. Unforgiving and relentless."

And yet, after each sick time away, she returns happy and

ready to take up where she left off, never mind that she spent the weekend in the hospital, an IV in her arm, surrounded by twinkling machines watching and listening to her every move; and, by the way, anybody who was interested could be given a tour of the bruises on her arm, not to mention a quick glance at the hospital wrist band that she still wore.

Truth be told, Dr. Crane is happiest when unwell, on the verge of having one of her shenanigans. It's almost as if this constant unwellness is one of her favorite places to visit, and whenever her shenanigans swoop in to strike, she hurriedly shuffles off to her office. Her shenanigans are notorious for attacking during Assessment meetings or Accreditation gatherings. That glazed look in her eyes, two hands on the tabletop, and before you know it, she is aiming for the door.

At first, I thought it was some sort of literary osmosis: having read too much Jane Austin and Charlotte Bronte, having been mesmerized by too many Victorian novels—consumption by another name. In her classes they tell me her students are sadly indifferent. She seesaws back and forth across the front of the classroom, caring nothing for white boards, PowerPoints, videos, any sort of razamatazza is out of the question, as she tosses her Sense and Sensibility lecture against the walls, tucking it neatly in between chairs and tables, bouncing it off the back windows, lecturing to an audience beyond mere college students. Until suddenly, her time up, she stops, and seeing there are rows of young people sitting, watching, waiting, she, they tell me, is surprised to see anybody in the same room with her.

But never mind because I am at the rim of her office door when I hear her say, "beastly." There is no context, nothing surrounding it, just 'beastly'. I have no choice but to peek—half a face at the door. She is alone, arms akimbo, staring at the many books in her bookcase. I dare not go any farther but wait for her to say more; when she doesn't, dropping her arms in some sort of annoyance, I hurry away over the gravy-colored carpet.

There are no students at my door—the coast is clear—and I quickly enter. That is the second time today I have thought of the coast being clear—the first earlier this morning as I rushed to take an empty elevator to the fifth floor, jabbing at the button before others could come. I wonder what it means, this coast is clear—something about pirates or smugglers, the weather? Following Simon's lead I shut the door and lock it. The locking part is important because they have a habit of knocking and entering, the knocking having nothing to do with waiting for an invitation. Sure enough it isn't long before there is a knock and a twist of the doorknob. Another knock, another twist. My hallway window is not like Simon's; there are no slits to peer through, no gaps. It is then, waiting to see if there will be yet another twist, that my reading glasses slip off my nose, bouncing at my feet. I need to fix this, but not sure how. Of course I could always invest in one of those straps, harnessing my glasses to my face, but something about that is horsey and all wrong and I would rather have them tumble off my face.

That night I have a dream, and it is green and hot and somewhere far away: a wet heat with blue-black jungle and wrist-thick vines. I turn in my sleep, even slide my hands under the pillow to look for cool, but the heat follows me everywhere. When I wake it feels like a short dream but I am sweating, hair wet, shower-like. I am exhausted. Looking at the clock and forgetting it is Saturday, the weekend, I see it is time to get up. I can't help but feel something like a good weakness, like after a sickness—all used up and thinner, lighter, and wonderfully empty.

That first dream of jungle followed me all that day and into the next. It was like no dream I'd ever had; the others are almost always fresh and clear in the morning, and I remember everything about them as I stand in the shower, the hot water pelting my face; but as the mornings wear on these other dreams grow weak, weaker, fading, until finally nothing by afternoon. But this jungle dream is different, growing bigger, and later, in the middle of the day, I remember something brand new about it: the way a fistful of bright yellow birds flickered in and out of the creepers, the jungle holding them like a friendly cage. By Sunday afternoon, new and exciting details continue to fall into place.

🙚🙚🙚

I really shouldn't be thinking about my jungle dreams in the middle of the day, not when students are lined up at the door, sitting on the floor, clustered around the podium because they need to take the course to graduate, to get their degree, to get jobs, to make money, to… Still, I step to the window and let them wait. There is a mumbling, heads turning to see the big clock on the wall behind them, faces staring down into cellphones. But I continue looking out the window, into the dusty trees of February, seeing nothing like my dreamy yellow birds. The third-floor windows are fine squares of glass that are not meant to be opened because the building has central air and why would anyone need to open a window. As I press a fingertip to the glass, a small unimportant brown bird flies to the ledge; it hops, maybe twitters and then, done with both, blurs away. In the end, I have looked far too long and they are restless and so I turn and go to the board and write my name and talk about things that all teachers talk about the very first day of class. I give them copies of a syllabus that are filled with directions, guidelines and rules. Secretly they like this. I neglect talking about grades, but towards the end they can't help but demand more information about numbers, letters, percentages. Some backward-capped young man in the back, beneath the clock asks, "How long do these papers have to be? How many words?" I tell them not to worry—later, but not the first day of class. They do not like answers like this, I can tell. A shuffling of feet, heads craning to see how much time is left. Two cellphones go beep, buzz, and each time I wait until their alarms stop.

∾∾∾

Later, office door unlocked, Maryam, John's grade appealer, finds me. I remember Maryam's face, having spoken with her before about other undeserving grades, wayward professors, and 'by the way, there's not enough room in the parking lot, not enough space. How can I make it to class on time in a situation like that? How can any of us? Please, tell me.' And yet, Maryam is surprisingly timid and for some reason thinks the words 'really' or 'just' are an important fixture to every sentence she utters.

"Hello, Maryam."

"You remember me, sir?"

"Certainly."

"Excuse me, sir, but I'd really like to know about the grade appeal. I'm just curious: is there a decision yet?"

"No, no, I spoke to Professor Redmann earlier today and nothing yet. If the two of you can't agree on a solution, it will go to a college committee, as per policy."

I am almost certain Maryam does not know what the word 'per' means but never mind; as department chair it has become a handy term, part of every administrator's legalese; it sounds extra important, and hints that whatever is to come won't be my fault.

"You know, I really don't want to cause any trouble; I really don't but he was so unfair, don't you think? So unfair and even rude, disrespectful, and both of these things together really bother me. You can understand that? Anybody can, *sah*?"

"Of course, of course." Hoping that will be the end of it, but then she takes a chair, and I cringe, wondering why I don't have a meeting to go to, a class to teach, some dental appointment I am late for. I shuffle through the papers on my desk in search of a misplaced memo, anything that would signal a retreat. Turning to look out the window might help: the city is shrouded in a dirty vanilla mist, something like dust and smog, but smaller, less important; by noon, the smog will blow out into the Gulf, leaving only dust and sand. However, until then…

"It's just that he never even looked at my medical excuses. He was really mad that I even offered him the papers. This, professor, is just not the way to deal with students, with anybody, this disrespect. Even I know this."

"Yes, yes, you are not wrong. I see your point," thinking that should do it, and any minute now she will take that last long look at her reflection in my window and leave, but... "And one more thing. . ." arms folded across her chest, ". . . one more thing, I think he treated me that way just because I am a girl. That's another complaint, and something I really should have added. A girl. Can you understand, professor?"

"Absolutely, totally uncalled for, totally." And with that I get up, stretch an early morning stretch and step toward my door, announcing, "Well, Maryam, I really must be going to a meeting now. So good to see you and good luck with the appeal."

Surprisingly, when she looks to be offering me her hand, I reach out and shake it, and just as surprisingly, she yanks it back, whispering, "You shouldn't do that, really you shouldn't."

That night there is a student concert by the Music Department: assorted drummers, guitar players, a trio of violinists, and one fearless saxophonist, all eager to display their new talents. I am sure they mean to play tunes we all know, have heard somewhere, but the only one I recognize is *Twinkle Twinkle Little Star*, and it is, of course, horrid, but we applaud as if it isn't. Henry Acer, Chair of Accounting and infamous storyteller of what life was like in the 1970's, sits next to me and is especially loud, almost seal-like, with his applause. When he catches me glancing his way, he leans over and mumbles, "A bloody screech-fest."

Later, at home, Peter calls to say, first, "Hello," and second, "Just to let you know that I need to cancel classes tomorrow."

As a rule, I don't ask why when it comes to things like this, but for Peter I often make exceptions. "And why is that, Peter?"

I have caught him off guard, unprepared, and I hear him clear his throat, maybe even take a moment to enjoy a sip of his secretive whiskey that everyone whispers about, before giving the sort of response that is usually reserved for student talk: "It's personal." Answers like this leave little room for additional questions, for meddling, we all know this.

Peter Wilson is two things: a Milton book that has been in the making for almost ten years, what he calls his project, and an academic who is constantly reminding all that he is first and foremost a Doctor, of the PhD variety, and second, a Professor: 'The name is Dr. Wilson, please, Dr. Wilson.' Students will nod in agreement and address him as Dr. Peter.

"Ok, I'll have Reedah put a notice on your classroom doors. By the way," . . . and here I purposely insert a lengthy pause—*do I hear the glassy tinkle of ice cubes?*—"By the way, how goes the project?"

The sense of relief on his end is palpable; we have successfully lurched away from the personal, moving into friendlier, well-worn terrain, and so, "Yes, it's about done, not long now. In fact, I sent a query to a couple of publishers last term. Yes indeed, as they say, I see light at the end of the tunnel." There is a longer pause, until he whispers, "'This horror will grow mild, this darkness light.'"

I pause back, until "Shakespeare?"

"Never. *Paradise Lost.*"

"Ah, of course."

The morning is full of people stopping by my office to unload their maladies, assorted tales of sorrow and unhappiness; and I listen, nodding at the appropriate time, tsking when necessary. Because she has a shuffle to her walk—as if her high heels are still practicing the stuff of stepping—I can hear her coming down the hallway. As a rule, she does not come to my office—to any of our offices—unless it is official dean business. She passes by as if she is headed somewhere else, somewhere bigger, more important, but it is an old ploy and in no time, she returns, slanting in the doorway, asking, "How goes it, Martin?"

I pretend surprise and say, "Oh, Hello. Fine, and you, Rose?"

"Could be better," shrugging. This, I know by now, is an invitation, and she waits to see if I accept.

"How's that?"

Re-shrugging, "Oh, you know, this accreditation business is killing me. Same story, different players, nobody wants to get in-volved, too busy, can't make meetings, doctors' appointments, or the always popular: personal reasons. Worse than students, this bunch."

I can see she is thinking about taking a seat, but when I bark a laugh, she changes her mind.

"What's so funny?"

I offer her an open hand. "Don't know. There must be a laugh in there somewhere. It doesn't change, *sah?*"

She winces at my *sah*. Having never stopped slanting in my doorway, hands at her waist, cowgirl-like, she says, "Oh, by the way, may I take a quick glance at your 3:30 class rooster?"

There are files and papers and books arranged in small towers on my desk and I glance at them before answering, "Sorry, what?"

"Your rooster for the class. I need to take a quick glance at it, just for a moment. Nothing serious, mind you, just one student, nothing to worry about."

I could invite her to take a seat, but don't. "The rooster?"

"Sure." And she takes a big step into my office.

It is a bright windy morning, with batches of students huddled here and there, as if double-daring the wind to ruin their day. Someone somewhere is whistling. And so, the dilemma has arrived: how does one go about correcting the dean's pronunciation? Most of us would say never mind, she's the dean and can do what she wants, while others would insist that I need to do her a favor, bring it to her attention, it's for her own good and in the end, she will thank me, etc. Still others will maintain that we know what she means and leave it at that.

Truth be told, she is notorious for her many mispronunciations. If not roster then dag for dog, koot for cute and so on. She has been known to end all-faculty meetings with the song "Row, Row, Row Your Boat" urging all of us to join in one last time. "Raw, raw, raw your boa..."

We arrived at the same time, some twelve years ago, Rose and I; she is tall, slim and insists on wearing high heels, making her even taller, slimmer. Although I am not a psychologist,

I can only imagine what it all means, these high heels, taking her higher yet. *Thinking of Icarus?* It is only right that after eight years of endless committee work along with tactful administrative maneuvering that she be appointed dean, with dreams of some-day being upgraded to a bigger and bolder deanship, or beyond. None of us know where this came from, this Rowing song, or even how it might fit into the world of university faculty and Tuesday afternoon meetings. At first her Rowing was met with disbelieving silence, a sprinkling of snickers and giggles. But, after meeting number three or four and the Rowing song still major part of the agenda, we slowly but surely joined in and sang it with her. Raw, raw, raw your boat/Gently down the stream/Merrily, merrily, merrily/Life is but a dream."

"The roster? You want to see my Raw-ster?" I say in a learning way.

But she is not the dean for nothing and pays me little attention.

Of course I simply nod and push the 3:30 class file her direc-tion, knowing full well that she will go through life saying rooster when she means roster, when I could have made a valiant effort to put a stop to it here and now but I didn't; and so she leaves my office, announcing, "Be right back," the class rooster firmly in her hand, the clip-clop of her high heels taking her back to her office at the other end of the building.

With a lull in the traffic, I walk to the first-floor Diner to buy a cup of their coffee. It comes from a fat silvery machine that hisses, huffing and puffing what I can only hope is some kind of steam. In the end, I am handed coffee with foam. As I walk off, coffee in hand, I catch a glimpse of Charles in the kitchen. Charles is the biggest, blackest man on campus and today he is wearing his white chef cap and looking intensely down at something on the countertop. I slow to see what it can possibly be. Finally all becomes clear: he is separating slices of cheese, lining them up in neat yellow squares, readying them for the cheeseburger lunch rush. I watch him until he looks up and waves, and although I wave back, there is something all wrong with big black Charles with chef hat separating thin slices of yellow cheese—one at a time, one at a time.

That afternoon a sandstorm rolls in off the Gulf. I had watched it most of the morning sitting out there, fidgeting, undecided. They say it has something to do with the monsoons in India, or perhaps the Americans churning up the desert with their heavy military equipment. Either way it is not to be liked. At the window, with diner-machine coffee in hand, watching the storm make up its mind, I hear an 'Excuse me' behind me, at my door; I turn to see an *abayaed* student. If one 'excuse me' weren't enough, she repeats, "Excuse me," and before she can say it yet again, I answer, "Yes?"

"Excuse me but where is Dr. Peter? His classroom is empty, and he's not in his office."

I offer the sandy Gulf one final glance before saying, "His class is cancelled today. Isn't there a note on the door?"

"I don't know, I didn't look."

"There should be a note."

All the while she hasn't stopped staring at my mouth, as if there is something all wrong with my lips and teeth; when she frowns and turns ever so slightly to look out my window, at the approaching sandstorm, I give my mouth a good rub to get rid of whatever it is.

"You know, he should email us like other professors. They all do it. If class is cancelled it should be done this way, don't you think?"

I answer, "Yes," wondering if there is enough room for me to squeeze by her and into the hallway, but she and her *abaya* are no match for me; they claim the doorway, caring nothing about moving. "Sad to say, Dr. Peter is not the most computer literate among us."

"*Nam*, but a professor, any person, should know how to email. Even my grandfather of 83 can do this."

A large mole has been perfectly placed between her eyes, giving her a third eyedness that I am unprepared for. She decides to smile—milky white teeth, wrapped in black *abaya*—and I stop to think what more I can say about Peter, in his defense, my mouth working, the words all lined up and ready to jump out, but, at the last moment, changing my mind and instead, "I think he knows how to email."

She shrugs at this, and we both wait.

But then, "By the way, it's raining but not raining," she announces.

Although I nod a nod that has nothing to do with agreement,

I wait for there to be more, some correction on her part. But she only smiles and scratches her chin. And so, "It is raining but not raining?" I question.

"Yes," the smiling gone but the scratching not.

I secretly consider this; it is a charming sentence, something a post-modernist or some wayward philosopher might utter, but of course I must not let her know this, and when I chance a glance out the window, I see the ground is in fact still damp from a morning rain, even though a dusty sun now blares down like a better idea. Meanwhile, I think about how to correct her, how to do my professorial duty. But before I can make things right, she continues, "Well, I must be going. It was good speaking to you, and if there is no class my driver is waiting," motioning in the direction of drivers; and with that she turns, heading into her raining but not raining day. All the while I say nothing, allowing her to believe that all is well, that, yes, it is raining but not raining.

I lean out of my office door to watch her go, and before she reaches the corner, stepping into the gaping elevator, she turns to wave good-bye, the kind of wave reserved for relatives at the airport. Once the elevator takes her, I move back to the window, looking five floors down, watching, waiting, for her to leave the building. When she appears—the only *abaya*—she is surrounded by the morning's lingering wetness, while the edge of the Gulf continues to churn a dirty blur. For the smallest moment I worry that this student of Peter's will go back into her world believing her sentence about rain is correct. I should have set her right. Sending young people into the world uncorrected cannot be good. Yet, the more I think about it, the more right she might be; in Los Angeles or perhaps Paris or even Seoul, somewhere it is most certainly raining right now. So, technically, she is not wrong—'raining but not raining'. And with that I feel better. Although I can no longer see her, by now I am sure her driver has picked her up and she is safely on her way home through the sunny-wet-growing-dusty streets.

ھھھ

Her name is Nasreen but will answer to Nancy. In fact, only her Arabic friends call her Nancy.

"It's kinda funny, don't you think? Even something like irony. Is that the word? Irony?"

Although her hair is long and black, secretly I think there is no such thing as black-black hair; there is always that tinge of brown, that aura of henna when the sunlight hits it just right. But Nasreen is different; her hair is black. I try her from different angles, standing so the biggest and brightest window is behind her, catching her in the glare of an afternoon yellow, watching intently as she brushes strands away from her cheeks; it squirrels around her neck, coils girlie around her ear, and every time it is black—a nighttime jungle black. It flows past the soft curve of her shoulder blades, not even bones, more like wings of flesh peek-a-booing through the glistening blackness.

It is the third class session, maybe the fourth of the new term but on a Wednesday for sure; and once everyone has filed out of the classroom, it is just the two of us because she stays behind, pretending to be looking for something in her bag, something that refuses to be found. Finally giving up her search, she looks up and is softly surprised to see me still there but since I am she says, "Do you know Basra?"

"Yes, I know of it."

"My home, my village, is up north," pointing up, "in the desert, not far from Basra."

I nod.

On this day, the Wednesday of her telling me that she is from Iraq, she has done something new with her hair; she's put it up and over into something like a fold in the back; it glistens doubly, and when I look for some kind of band or pin holding it all together, I see none.

"Sometimes I am homesick, you know. Homesick. Yes, of course I like this place," using both hands to show me this place and how she likes it. "But it's not the same. Fewer friends, bigger and better cars. They laugh harder here. Can I say that? Harder?"

"What is the name of your home, your village?"

This surprises her, and her eyes grow big, bigger, and she stops to think, tilting her head puppy-like. "It's a small, unimportant village. You would not know it. Nobody knows it except those who live there, and even some of them would like to forget, I think. It doesn't matter. Just some village in the middle of the desert, with a river over there, some train tracks over here, Basra, 150, maybe 160 kilometers that way." Pointing through the window, into the brightness of February.

"I have to go now," she says.

"Yes."

"I have another class and I don't want to be late."

"Of course. Until next time."

2

In the morning I almost always have a cup of coffee and jam on toast. Later, when I am thinking of other things—looking up and to the right, as if there is something to be read in that corner of the ceiling—I can't remember what I had for breakfast, or even if I ate at all, but I must have and it must have been coffee, toast with jam because that is what I always have. For lunch I have a sandwich, salami and cheese, ice water, for dinner, another sandwich, less cheese, more salami. Of course she cooks and there are other foods, but later, perhaps when they are asleep, I will move through the house, down the stairs, into the kitchen and have my sandwich.

Wednesday mornings are extra quiet because the daughters go to school, she to work and I have no classes until mid-morning. Looking at the dog look back at me through the screen door, sipping coffee, its steam working on my face and considering Nasreen, her hair, and then—the dog scratching at the screen, now jumping, showing the pink of its belly—remembering the day the second daughter was born, how the same dog, smaller, pinker, scratched at that same screen, whining, when somebody's cousin, maybe nephew, said, "Another girl? Too bad, heh?" All the while shaking my hand, grinning.

The next dream is of a grove in that same jungle. It is mist-filled, followed by a double black of jungle and then an evening sky bristling with stars and planets. The moment the dream starts, the sweating begins, the damp hollow of the pillow; but like before I feel good and used and when a breeze finds its way through the trees, it makes everything extra cool, even cold. Like all such dreams, I have no idea why I am there in the jungle, how I arrived; there is a hum in the trees. In this dream, it is understood I am to wait, to sweat, and to watch the mist swirl. The humming throbs like a pulse while the mist grows thin, thinner, gone.

"What's the matter?"

"What?"

"Are you sick?"

"Sick?"

"You're soaked. Fever? Cold? What?"

"No, maybe it's the blankets."

"The blankets?"

She yawns, stretches and moves toward the bathroom. Running my hand through wet sticky hair, I never thought of it as sickness, not once.

The next time I see John he is standing in the hallway, hands behind his back, looking up at the ceiling as if there's something special there. I walk over next to him so we can look up together:

a dimpled moonscape, one tile after another. Finally, speaking straight up, he says, "And so?"

I continue to look, wondering what he possibly can be so-ing about.

"So?"

Done looking up, his face a small red around the ears, he says, "Yes, and so what's with the grade appeal?"

For some reason I am relieved that it is only that.

"I tried to convince her that there was nothing to it, that it would be denied, that all the signs were there, denial, that…"

"But?"

"But she insisted; 'this disrespectfulness cannot stand,' I believe were her words. At any rate, she did the paperwork and everything's now in the committee's hands."

He nods to this. "And who's on the committee?"

I pull at my ear because his ears are still a bright red, and look back at the ceiling as if their names are written there, on the tiles.

"Oh, there's Rebecca and Thompson from History and Accounting Jeremy, and . . ."

"Jeremy…?"

"Yes, and …."

Jeremy Wilkenson? Not Jeremy Wilkenson?" His hands coming out from behind his back, redirecting his eyes to look me full in the face.

"Yes, and …"

"Jeremy Wilkenson is a notorious lover of students' rights and freedoms, everybody knows this. He is simply mystified with them, unwilling to unhinge himself from the 60s: Black Panthers, SDS, Abbie Hoffman. Christ. I don't have a chance, Christ. *Quia caritas Dei.*"

And with that John marches off toward his office, softly clicking the door shut behind him.

Although grade appeals are nothing, everybody wants to be liked, loved, even John the Medievalist, maybe especially John. If John stays true to form, he will miss the next department meeting, refuse to answer emails, and call in sick two maybe three times before the end of the month. Meanwhile, post-John, but still standing in the hallway, out in the open, Marshall is suddenly at my side.

When I first met Marshall Mullen four, . . . no five years, ago, he made it a point to tell me after his interview, in private, washing our hands in the bathroom together, that, 'Dr. Martin, I am ready and ripe for your department. You can see that, right?' Leaning closer, staring into the garbage basket together, 'Mr. Chairman, FYI, I'm not afraid of anything, not a thing.' This, of course, was the stuff of the Boy Scouts, Tom Swift, Teddy Roosevelt. Now, five years later, here he is at my side, grinning, whispering, "What are you doing out in the open like this? Like one of those wildebeests caught on the savannah all alone. What's the occasion?"

I tell him there is no special occasion but he doesn't believe it. "No, No," his grin never wavering, "I don't believe it."

Marshall has a tattoo that covers his entire right arm—something about two dragons intertwined, warring against an array of demons and hellish creatures. It's all very intricate and greenred—from wrist to shoulder. And so, he makes a point of wearing short-sleeved shirts to show it off whenever he can, and if people don't stop and stare, ask what it means, 'didn't it hurt?' he's annoyed, insisting it only serves to support his lifelong thesis that people are dull, indifferent and 'sadly fearful of anything that might smack of adventure.' Last spring there was a movement afoot to have Marshall replace me as chair. Almost everyone thought it was a good idea except Marshall. "I have no desire to play the amateur psychologist with faculty, students and disgruntled parents. No thank you. It simply is not worth the stipend and course release," rubbing his dragons as if this had been some sort of group decision, he and his dragons—the one dragon's snarl beginning to sag at the elbow.

When we interviewed Marshall, he was right, we liked him right away, all except Sara, who, I recall, insisted 'something not right here'. His publications were top notch: a handful of clever articles on why Leslie Fiedler was all wrong, about oh so many things. We were all secretly looking forward to having a Marshall in the department; and yet, up until the very shortlist end, Sara held firm to her 'something not quite right here' attitude.

Returning to my office, I find people sitting there, in my chairs, uninvited. He offers me no chance for a Good morning, Hello, not even a What can I do for you, before, "So this English 100 class, this . . . what? . . ." spinning his hands like he knows something about twirling, maybe even some magic tricks, ". . . developmental writing class cannot be right for Saba. My sister needs something more challenging, something bigger, better, you understand. Her teachers have called her superior. Since elementary school, level one, they have called her superior."

Before he can continue, the cellphone that he had so neatly placed on the table, to his right, next to the swirl of prayer beads, twinkles and jingles, and the best he can do is grab it, turn sideways and talk into my window with a view of the Gulf. Together we—what I imagine can only be Saba, and me—wait for him. She twice runs her fingers around the rim of her *hijab,* searching for anything that might be loose, out, dangling. Meanwhile, not once has he allowed the caller a chance to respond, to say yes, no, or maybe; he is, in fact, one long line of gruff Arabic. Saba turns to look into the hallway, where two girls are talking and giggling. Finally he snaps the phone shut, says, "Excuse", straightens his *dishdasha,* hands on tabletop. He has a fine moustache and a finer watch. He on my left, she on my right.

His handshake is weak, almost unimportant, even out of practice, but I have learned that that doesn't mean anything, not the way it used to.

"She has always earned good marks, you see," motioning toward Saba. "This one, always a good student, everybody says so."

I turn to her, asking, "Tell me about some of the things you have written: essays, stories, maybe some poetry? Perhaps you have brought some samples for me to look at?"

"Yes, Saba's written all of these things, and more. She's the best, I tell you, number one." Thumbs up like an astronaut.

All the while, except to perfect her *hijab,* she hasn't taken her fingers away from her lips, not once, only nodding. He picks up his prayer beads, sits back in the chair and sighs like this is work, this talking to professors about his sister's writing, and he needs a break, some kind of second wind. The giggling girls have moved on, farther down the hallway, and in their place is a boy, books at his chest, waiting his turn. That's when I hold up the paper that has her placement score. "Saba, is it?"

"Yes."

"Saba, unfortunately your test score is not very good. It says you should take this English 100, this developmental class. You know, students take placement tests for a reason; the purpose of such tests is not to punish but to help, to . . ." I am not so sure I still believe these old arguments, but never mind, I talk to her as if I do.

Surprisingly, she looks directly at me, her fingers leaning to the right, and says, "Yes, I see." But then I make the mistake of glancing his way, and quickly, as if he feels there is a tide of sorts and it is turning against him, he cups his prayer beads in both hands—his break now over—leans forward, saying, "Yes, she understands what placements tests are. We all understand, but I tell you she is ready for this other course, this credit course, this more advanced 101 class."

I look to see if she agrees, but there are only fingers at the lips and blinking.

"You see, I've studied in the States, MBA Maryland, you know the Fighting Terps?" This last part bringing his biggest, best smile. "So I have seen this good writing you are talking about, many times—maybe hundreds of times. I have done it myself. I know what you are looking for; we all know, and this one has it. Saba...," motioning toward her as if she is more than just a tabletop away, "came to visit me once—remember?" She nods yes, she remembers. "My first year at College Park—remember?" Nodding that she still remembers. "Anyway, let's come back to this..." placing his hand in the center of the table and dragging it slowly toward himself, "this writing test, this placement test." Taking a deep breath, "Professor, sometimes these tests don't tell the truth, you see. Sometimes, in their own way they lie, or only tell part of what is true, *sah*? This is the case with this one, Saba. Your tests don't tell the whole truth. She does not need this non-credit English 100. She is ready for the other, the credit, the bigger class."

"Are you?"

"Yes," he says.

"Are you?"

"Yes, Saba, please tell the professor. Please explain to him how this English 100..." looking quickly to his left, then right, as if the English 100 class were here a moment ago, but now, when he wasn't looking, disappeared. "...is not for you."

Again letting her fingers curl away from her lips for just a moment and when she does, I can see that her teeth are almost perfect: white, straight across. In a whisper she says, "Yes, what my brother tells you is true. All true."

"See. There it is. See, just like I said." Smiling first at his hands, then at me, as if 'There, it's done, settled. Nice talking with you'.

The boy with textbooks at his chest is still waiting, looking sadly at me, at my name on the door, as if whatever it is it is not his fault, and yet here he is, what can he do; and I turn to her and recommend that she take the development class, English 100.

"Recommend." He snatches at the word. Although it sounds like a question, it really

isn't. "Recommend. Is this the word I'm hearing? Recommend?"

"Yes, recommend, . . ."

"Fine," pushing back, rising, holding out his hand for one final shake. "Fine, recommend. You hear that, Saba, recommend."

She nods and hurries to stand up, and now out of nowhere she too has a cellphone that needs talking to.

Even though he is standing, moving toward the door, cellphone at the ready, he goes on and I nod like he is talking wisdom, but I have heard it all before, if not from older brothers, then from well-read mothers, used-to-getting-their-way fathers, uncles who own construction companies, car rentals, shopping centers.

જ્જ્જ્

That afternoon, just when I think the coast is clear—I am sure it has something to do with pirates, maybe bootleggers—Khalid is at the door.

Khalid has been with us for six, no seven years. Contrary to conventional wisdom and hallway gossip, Khalid is not stupid; he simply understands that graduation will not be to his benefit. As a result, he purposely fails classes so he will have to take them again and again, all the while toying with academic probation. There is talk that the Egyptian army eagerly awaits his graduation, that he has dodged his two-years of military service for too long. His name is on a list. Khalid is all about drama. He's always the first to volunteer to read in class, raising his arm soldier straight. When Achilles slew Hector at the gates of Troy, he gave one of his best performances. We applauded. Front-row Amal wiped away her tears as Khalid's mighty Achilles towed Hector's body through the Trojan dust. After class, he came to me, wondering, "Was it ok?" I said it was.

So, this is the Khalid at the door, or no, his head is at the door, peeping in, somber and nothing at all like the drama I remember.

"Yes, Khalid?"

"He did it again."

"He did?"

"*Nam.*"

"Tell him to stop it."

"Can I?"

This is all part of our six-year play; of course, I have no idea what he is talking about and he knows it.

"Dr. James, he did it again."

I sigh, which means I give up and he wins this time.

"He won't let me leave class to pray. He says we have a quiz, and I said it's time for prayers and will only be gone five minutes, even less. But he said no. And I said yes. What do you say?"

"I say no."

Khalid stops, until "Which way is that a no?"

"A no to you."

"You refuse to let me pray?"

"Pray if you want but stepping in and out of the classroom for any reason, cannot be a good idea. Right?"

"You don't trust me, is that it?"

This is one of his many dramatic questions, but I am ready for it. "Khalid, I trust you, I am sure we all trust you but other students I might question, you can see that, right?"

"But we are talking only about me, not others. Me."

I wonder if he has been rereading his Hamlet, maybe Richard the Third.

"Yes, yes, but others will see and if we let you go, . . . see where I'm going with this?"

Khalid, being secretly smart, knows I would say this; even before he stepped into my office, he knows. He pretends that he does not like my answer and will head to the dean's office to complain. He fingers the door frame as if, suddenly, its wood is so very important. Finally, he says in his biggest and best reading voice, "I have to go, I have an appointment."

"Good-bye, Khalid."

"Maybe."

∾∾∾

Nasreen raises her hand while others blurt out answers, half answers, thinking this is what big learning is all about. All the while her hand remains straight, tall, waiting to be called upon no matter what. And I cannot help but wonder if she knows Khalid, they went to the same arm-raising school. I call on her and she does her best to explain. When she stops to fumble over the right word, two others jump in to fill the quiet, but when I hold up my hand like some traffic cop they stop; meanwhile, Nasreen has found the right word and it is 'regardless'. When class is finished, she is the last to leave, the only one to wave good-bye, and I find myself waving back.

That evening my daughters squabble over sweaters. Although I spend the evening aimed at the TV, I hear everything they say.

"Green is my color, you know. Always has been. My favorite color."

"Fine, but this is one is more blue than green. Even I can see that. Blue."

I dream of rotting palm fronds bunched snake-like around trees, the sweet stench of decay wafting across the jungle floor. As I sit on a rock lined with furry moss, the odor climbs off the ground and like a thing with legs, quickly finds my feet, my thighs, trickling across my chest and into my face and nose, bringing tears. I shake my head, shuffle my feet but a smell like this will have its way, worming up through the leaves and vines and black earth, filling the long fingers of sunlight.

In the morning, I wake to voices still arguing over clothes, this time shoes.

At the elevator—me going in, he coming out—I pass Ahmad. Because he is in his normal early-morning rush, he only has time to squeeze out a "Morning."

Not to be outdone, I counter with, "Good morning."

Ahmad Ahmed is intelligent, Jordanian, and knows his literary theory; he came to us from the University of Chicago amid great fanfare. To look at Ahmad you would think he would be more attune to children's literature, the poetry of Rod McKuen, *The Bridges of Madison County*. He insists on wearing brightly colored bow ties, with a belt that is Texas big and long, hanging unlooped in the front so it flaps when he walks. Ahmad likes purple shirts, if not purple then something like a deep-sea blue. At department meetings Ahmad is, as a rule, always the last to arrive and the first to leave; coming in, he will routinely slouch his way over to me, apologizing profusely as he approaches, until, hugging what appears to be an armful of student papers, he bends to tell me why he is late, and then, even closer, whispers, "Sorry, but I'm afraid I must leave in twenty minutes because. . . . During Ahmad's fifteen minutes of meetingness, he will spend his time cleaning his fingernails, petting the hair on his wrists, and every now again, sneaking peeks at Sara, who, I am certain, does not even know his name. As long as I have known Ahmad, he has had a hint of a moustache, a ragged line of black hairs. I worry that for some exotic Jordanian reason he grooms his moustache that way.

The next morning there seems to be some unfriendliness going on in the parking lot; a knot of students and security, white-shirted Nepalese armed with cellphones, hover by the tennis courts. There's yelling, followed by laughter, followed by a bigger, angrier yelling. The white-shirted Nepalese are watchful, holding on tight to their cellphones. I alter my walk to visit the fray, and when I get there, I am disappointed because it is nothing more than an argument over cars; one student has parked too close to another's Lamborghini. It is a dull argument and what makes it at all interesting is that the two sides have, as usual, called their assorted friends and cousins to come support their side of the argument. Both sides arrive surprisingly quick, and there is much smoking of cigarettes and hands in pockets until, in the end, the student who parked too close to the Lamborghini gingerly backs up his car and reparks, and everybody is happy, handshakes all around. The white-shirted Nepalese security re-holster their cellphones and wander off. Cousins and friends linger until, eventually, the two sides discover they are not done yet: one is a Real Madrid supporter the other Barcelona. The Nepalese stop to rethink about returning.

That afternoon, out of nowhere, a gang of tall mushrooming clouds churn in out of the north, bringing with it a heavy downpour, which takes us all to the windows. Heavy rain will make the front page in tomorrow's newspaper.

છ૭છ૭છ૭

For lunch Peter is eating popcorn and when I ask him why, he answers like somebody's five-year-old, "Because."

Willing to give him a second chance, I walk off to inspect the copy machine, make a copy of my hand before moving on to the third floor to see if Ahmad is holding class. When he sees me peering through the small square of a prison window, I nod and he ignores me. I return to Peter. "Why the popcorn?"

This time he says, "Because today I feel like I'm at the movies.

Ever have one of those days, full of theatre, the magic of the silver screen?"

Wanting to be on his side, I answer, "I've had my moments."

"Ah," dropping a handful of popcorn into this mouth. "There you have it."

We both wait for his chewing to stop, for the popcorn to be gone.

"Some sort of drama in your 415 class? Something I should know about?"

"On the contrary, my dear captain, nothing like drama I am afraid, but comedy … High comedy, I think, or maybe low. Either way, comedy for sure. Regardless…," motioning to his bag of popcorn that is almost empty, "… I like popcorn."

"Comedy you say?" fidgeting in front of his desk like some anxious student, holding my elbows like I don't care. "How's that?"

He stops in mid-chew to ask, "Now is this a department chair asking or something else, someone else?"

Peter, who hates being called Pete, is like Sara, both think answering a question with a question is the modern way to converse. Sensing that there is something I should know, something he is holding back, I trump his question with, "Why should you care?"

"Right, why should I." I edge a little closer until I find myself leaning, sniffing his popcorn air to see if I should be smelling something else, something more. "Right. Why should I?"

Almost done now, about ready to arrive at an answer, just one more step. "What happened?"

"Actually it's my fault."

"How's that?"

"I told her once, twice, even a third time, can you imagine, three times, and she wouldn't turn it off, put it away, stop her secret messaging." Reaching into a bag that is now empty of popcorn, he smashes it into a hard papery ball. "And so, I had reached that point where enough is enough, don't you agree? We can only take so much, you and me, even here?" Motioning as if he is about to do a magic trick. "After all, we're in control, you and me, don't you think? In charge? This idea of respect that we hear so much about."

His barrage of questions all used up, I jump in, "What did you do?"

"Ah, there's the rub." Tossing his papery ball towards a waste-paper basket that I only hope is somewhere behind his desk. "I took her phone and threw it against the wall."

"You did?"

"I did."

"You broke it?"

"In oh so many colorful pieces."

When I returned to my office two missed calls from the President's office are waiting for me, one email marked Urgent.

"You've undoubtedly heard about Peter's misadventure by now."

"Yes, he called it comedy."

There is the shortest hint of a presidential silence that is only broken with something like a snort. "He thinks it's funny?"

"Comedy *sans* the humor, I think," I say.

"Is there such a thing?"

"There is, but it's called something else."

The president cannot see me shrugging, but I do and there is more silence.

Two days later, and after a flurry of emails and assorted meetings, Peter is given an official letter of reprimand, ordered to apologize to the girl, and pay for her broken machine. All of this is spelled out in a confidential letter that Peter signs in triplicate.

3

That weekend we head south, to one of the resorts. Once there, like always, they aim for the souks and malls, while I, waving good-bye, am content to enjoy poolside.

Looking down, seeing an ant carrying two blades of grass, one greener and shorter than the other, and knowing that I am the only person in the world, in any world, seeing this, I can only wonder what it plans to do with blades of grass that are three, no four times longer than it is. *Food? Something for the nest? Do ants even have nests? Is it a he or she or something else in the ant world? Can a petite female ant carry something that large?* In the universe of ants anything is possible. And of course, the ant, who is more brown than black, cares nothing for me, as it continues to drag the blades across what must only appear to it as a vast desert of concrete. When I look to see where it's headed, there is nothing like an ant home in sight, no crack in the cement, no bushes or flower bed—nothing that looks even remotely anty. In the middle of thinking about this—chin in hand—a woman in a blue dress comes up behind me, walks to the edge of the patio and yells out in what has to be Russian to her friend who is floating face up in the pool. But the face-up floater is not hearing so she places one high heel foot on the patio, dangerously close to the laboring ant, and uses a bigger, louder Russian, and when she does two things happen: the floater is startled out of floating and I see an errant red thread hanging from the hem of her blue dress. In a flurry of now sedate Russian, the two of them quickly agree on something because the blue dress woman with red thread dangling nods and goes back the way she came while the other returns to her floating. I have lost sight of the ant and when I look to see where it should be, there is nothing but dimpled concrete; looking farther, thinking wouldn't it be something if it had progressed that far in only thirty seconds of Russian, I scan ahead, and sure enough there it is, a flash of twitching green. I can't believe it has gotten that far that fast. Just then, leaning forward, squinting to get a better look, a gray-haired Grandpa with what can only be his grandson take their turn on the patio, strolling by, the little boy in the middle of asking, "Ok, but, Grandpa, why do you take so long brushing your teeth?"

And Grandpa, without hesitation, as if this is not a new question, answers, "My teeth are more complicated than yours. Old people's teeth are always that way, everybody knows that." The grandson smiling up at him, as if to say, 'Yes, that's correct.'

When the two of them step closer to the pool's edge, Grandpa takes his hands out of his pockets, and when he does the grandson now wonders, "What time is it?"

Grandpa, looking down at his wrist as if there is a watch there when there isn't, says, "Two-thirty."

The boy looking wide-eyed, even holding up a tiny hand to push back the sun, asking, "How did you do that?"

"What?"

"Tell me the time without a watch. How did you do that?"

Grandpa, sighing, whispers, "Practice."

Meanwhile, the Russian floater is out of the pool and holding a towel that is far too small for any swimmer. All done at the pool's edge, Grandpa with grandson turn as one and that is when I see something on the old man's elbow—something like an extra piece of skin or meat hanging from his elbow. But that can't be right. When he stoops to tell the grandson something about the concrete, bending and pointing, the whateveritis on his elbow flutters, and now I see it: a piece of leaf has found its way there, at his elbow, waving like somebody's tiny toy banner. Still bending, pointing, talking to his grandson, who hasn't stopped nodding, I expect the piece of leaf to fall away at any moment. After all, how long can a leaf cling to old, wrinkled flesh? But it seems at home, minding its own business. For the shortest moment, I think about calling out to Grandpa, warning him of a leaf that refuses to let go, but they are now done with their inspection of the concrete and make their way off the patio, turning right at the shrubbery. The Russian floater, towel firmly around her neck, standing arms akimbo, staring straight up into a bright blue sky. She is looking the wrong way to see a muffin-shaped cloud behind her, lingering as if freshly baked.

ॐ ॐ ॐ

In class I tell them about what I saw Saturday at poolside, and they—having been taught to be polite when it comes to teachers and assorted old people— wait for me to finish, until, finally, Hamad, who has told me more than once, secretly, like Marshall, that he is not afraid of anything, raises his hand, asking, "Excuse me, sir, but why are you telling us this…this about ants and Russians and old people with leaves on their elbows? Is this important? Part of the lesson? Some sort of special test material? Please sir, we need to know."

I sigh, and the best I can do is say, "It is important, but rest assured, it is not the material of quizzes or examinations. But …" holding up an index finger, "but, later, much later, things like this will be the most important of all."

In the first row, Fatemah looks up at me, regretfully, as if to whisper, 'It's ok everybody makes mistakes, and don't worry, I understand, they don't, I do.' Hamad nods, as if he has caught me doing something all wrong and now everybody knows. Hamad, who is not afraid of anything.

I smile back at Fatemah, appreciating her loyalty.

ॐ ॐ ॐ

Three days later, Peter, stepping quickly into my office, politely snapping the door shut behind him, tells me he apologized to her in private, in his office, while she, wearing a straight-ahead, gum-chewing stare, said nothing, and when he asked her how much the phone cost, he couldn't believe it was that expensive, but "I paid her anyway." When he asked for a receipt, he had to tell her what to write. Peter should have been fired. We all know this, all except the girl and her family. I ask him if this student will pass the course, and he says, "Of course. In fact, she's looking more and more like A material to me." He finishes quickly, in something like a grin, or maybe a grimace.

The next day, in bold letters the headlines announce that one of the important sheikhs has died, pushing the heavy rain story to page two. It goes on to say he was extremely popular because he knew how "to juggle west with east," had homes in Dubai, London, Istanbul, New York City and something like a villa in Muscat. Not only that but, it continues, "he had a sense of humor that served him well over these many years." He had been out of the public eye for quite some time, and when that happens with important sheikhs rumors spring up. Although he was only 63, the rumor said it didn't matter because he was still sick. And so, he has died and the only proper thing left to do is to mandate three days of national mourning. So decreed by the Amir.

There are three steps involved when this happens: first, there is general, genuine sorrow, those who knew him beating their breasts, tearful, wailing women covered in the blackest *abayas*; two, something like a bittersweetness sets in, a lingering sadness softly diluted with joy because for three days there will be no work, no classes, the roads full of cars hurrying to the chalets; and finally, for students, the not–so–fast step three because of course those three days of missed classes will have to be made up somewhere, sometime. Sure enough, before the end of the day, the official announcement comes from the president's office saying that 'the University wishes to express its profound sorrow in the passing of such an important national figure. May Allah rest his soul'; and oh, by the way, for the next three Saturdays in a row classes will have to be made up. "Thank you for your cooperation." All of which ignites a flood of emails from faculty and students, complaining about, among other things, institutional unfairness. Sara telephones saying she has already made plans for two of those Saturdays; Ahmad's email is quick to follow, insisting that a family reunion has been scheduled since September, food and cakes have been purchased, airline tickets on credit cards, etc. Marshall leaves a message on my telephone; "Really, Herr Chair?" To all of this I respond with, "Yes, I know. Noted."

Soon after I place my hand on the telephone to call the president, but when I can't remember why, I pull my hand away; and when I do almost immediately it rings. It is the president asking, "What do you want?"

ৰ৵ৰ৵ৰ৵

John is obsessed with the grade appeal. When I see him, I know he wants to know what I know about it, and the best I can do is hold up my best policeman-stopping-traffic hand, announcing, "I haven't heard a word. I will know when you know. It's in the committee's hands, John. Should be a ruling any day now. Have they asked you for more information, additional documentation?"

"No? Nothing."

"This may be a good sign, a clear-cut decision is on the way."

Although John nods, it is a nod of disbelief, a nod that says all you administrators are alike, something like the Masons but more bookish.

Not long after that the president calls, and after a chatty segment of useless small talk about rain, sandstorms and the price of oil, says that if another Peter episode occurs, he, 'unfortunately', will have no choice but to let him go, to "release Dr. Peter from his contract." He wants to say more and I can tell he is getting ready to use the word unfortunately again but before he can, I say, "I understand completely."

He was expecting something else, something more, and weakly responds with, "You do?"

"Of course." And just like that we are done.

❧❧❧

It's four steps between ceiling sprinkler heads. Although I am nothing like an engineer, nothing resembling a firefighter, even I can see that if a fire were to erupt in the far corner, between bookcase and window, that no sprinkler would have the watery gusto to dowse it. All of which makes me wonder about the odds of such a fire breaking out in such a dim corner of my office. *It could happen. Yes, it could, but unlikely. But it's possible. You have to admit that it is possible. Possible but highly improbable. Yes, but possible . . ,* and so on.

When I turn to look out over the Gulf, I see four, no five blue and white boxy container ships neatly lined up to enter the port.

Three at one time is unusual while four is unheard of. I wonder if anyone else sees what I see. Of course I have no way of knowing, and as I watch them shimmer in the dusty haze that forever lives on the horizon, I wonder who I can call to tell what I am seeing, who I can share this with? If I call home to share, I will be greeted with silence, or worse: 'Martin, really? Martin, please tell me you called for something else, anything else.' That's when there is yet another knock at the door.

The embassy sent out a message last night, rather late, that, in so many words, urges us to be careful, to not go out alone, to stay away from crowds, to tone down our Americanism, etc. We get messages every now and again from the embassy about this, especially when the weather begins to get cooler and more people are out and about to picnic, to walk, to enjoy their family in a sometimes-grassy park.

There is an all-faculty college meeting today; the dean's email says attendance is mandatory. We see this wording every now and again, and we have never discovered what it means or what happens if someone does not attend. The punishment remains a mystery. Sitting outside, getting ready for the meeting, I watch pigeons flap by, roosting in the shade of a window ledge. Sitting with a paper cup full of Diner coffee, not caring if I drink it or not, but at least there it is on the table, in front of me, just in case. Some research somewhere now says that too much hot coffee can cause throat cancer. Grabbing hold of the coffee, I give it a test sip and when it feels nothing like hot, I chance it and sip some more.

I watch an older man with what has to be his young wife walk by, pushing a baby stroller. He is old, she is not, and at another time, another place I might consider this, and even offer silent judgment, but now, these days, I am content to observe only. It is so much easier that way. My cellphone rings twice and I struggle to dig it out of my pocket. It's a message in Arabic, and although I can't read it, I am sure it has to do with wanting to sell me a new car, maybe, two, or how about a new mobile calling plan, or wait, interested in real estate in India? Repocketing the cellphone, I look to see where the old man with young woman and stroller have gone, and of course they are nowhere to be seen. Another sip of coffee but by now it is too cold to be any of good.

I go to the faculty meeting, sitting in the back, next to one of the exits. As feared, it is all about assessment and strategic planning, and there is even mention of accreditation, all offered in the eye-rolling jargon that is Janie Williams.

Janie Williams is—there are simply no other words for it—an assessment addict. She knows the terminology, talks the talk, and while the rest of us can only grimace and silently groan, opening newspapers to the sports page, toying with our cellphones, correcting papers, she continues on with such enthusiasm and relish that, quite frankly, it borders on the heroic. Janie's power points are notoriously clever and artsy. Unlike the rest of us, she does not believe in the dullness of simple bullet points but instead, she entertains with cartoons, swirling numbers and marching percentages. Her charts and graphs are exotic, leaning left or right, sometimes swaying. Her diagrams can speak French. Janie

Williams teaches computer science and is everybody's big sister, favorite aunt, mother on a good day. She has been known to read entire books on accreditation. Regardless, after fifteen minutes of Janie and her power point acrobatics, I wait for the appropriate time and when she hesitates, slows to double-check a percentage, I guiltlessly move toward the exit, into the hallway and back out into the pigeon-filled morning.

☙☙☙

Peter's Milton book has been accepted for publication. He tells me this in an official memo. I congratulate him in a return official memo. I must be sure to announce this at the next department meeting. If I forget or if the announcement lacks academic sincerity, he will silently punish me by cancelling classes, missing office hours. Call in sick.

"This is wonderful news, Peter."

"Yes, isn't it."

"I am so very happy for you."

"Yes, well, I'm happy for myself, too."

Peter has always been better at emails than telephone calls.

There is no wind today, which means the heat is flat and blaring and people walk into the building red-faced and unfriendly. It is a heat that has nothing to do with sunbathing, nothing recreational here. It is a hot that can hurt, drain you of moisture in moments. Tourists are hospitalized on days like this.

Later, as I step to the window to watch the cargo ships, I can see a slice of the parking lot and someone has brought his pet monkey and has it doing tricks on the hood of his car. Girls gather to point and giggle, to take photographs. He and his monkey are the center of attention for twenty minutes on a Wednesday afternoon. But even a monkey can only do so many somersaults on what must be a broiling-hot hood. He nibbles a handful of green apples before growing weary, seemingly defeated, thinking that even for a monkey, enough is enough. Actually, since the girls have now gone to class, he reels in his monkey and hands it over to his driver, who all the while has been sitting behind the steering wheel, with air-conditioning, watching through the window. The girls all gone, the driver neatly tucks the monkey in its cage and drives away. Meanwhile, the monkey-owner, cellphone at his ear and all alone, lazily saunters onto campus.

A windstorm wakes me up in the middle of the night. It whistles around the windows, the dust tumble-weeding down the street. The building creaks and moans. In the morning yellow jumpsuit workers are hard at work sweeping up the swirls of new sand on the sidewalks, along the streets. Garbage dumpsters lay wounded and broken on their sides, their rubbishy guts strewn across the street. Like always the sky is a crisp hard blue after such winds.

Sara, who never calls me calls me; she is not feeling well and will not be in today. I fight back the urge to ask for details but stop with, "Fine."

There is the smallest pause before she continues, "It can't be helped."

This sounds very un-Sara-like, almost like an invitation and so, 'Everything ok?"

That's all she needs to remember herself, ending with, "*Inshallah*, good-bye."

With last night's wind, the morning's messy street, and Sara's mindyourownbusiness good-bye, the day is on reset.

☙☙☙

Yousef is forever angry. He frowns at any and all assignments.

"How are you today, Yousef?"

"Tired."

"Impossible, you're too young to be tired."

I smile, he doesn't.

Yousef has pimples and something is wrong with his earlobes; they are impossibly broken, sticking out like wings. When he frowns, he looks like a face from one of those post office wanted posters. I have to turn away when Yousef decides to frown because if he sees me smirking, it will only make things worse. Yousef sits in the back, up against the window, his long dark hair kept in a tight, slick ponytail.

"You stayed up too late, heh?"

"Maybe."

Since Yousef is older than the others, maybe 26 or 27, his questions are often tough and double daring: "How do you know?" "Why is that important?" "Will that be on the test?" Yousef is the only one who knows what the word crenellate means.

Nasreen wears a necklace that is more red string and jade than necklace. At first, I think the jade is an animal—dragon, lion, some kind of horse—but now, after two weeks of looking when she isn't, I am convinced it's nothing more than a block of jade. She wears it so tight against her throat that it wobbles when she talks.

In the back, not far from Yousef, sit the lovers, their chairs angled so the edges touch. They are almost always smiling at each other. I don't mind them because they are in the back, say little and care nothing about the class. In fact, in a reminiscing way, I envy them; if envy is not the right word, then jealousy is. He wears a red baseball cap; she keeps her hair in braids every day, different ribbons, same braids. Although they are both failing the course, they have no cellphones; they spend fifty minutes looking at one another, whispering, sometimes giggling. I can't be angry with them.

The Diner is empty this early in the morning and I have one of their machine-hissing coffees with toast topped with two squares of coppery butter. Thinking of nothing but 8:00 am and coffee with toast, I look down and see *250 fils* on the floor, at my feet. I pick it up, turning it this way and that, before slipping it into my pocket. That's when a new perfectly round face that I don't recognize emerges from the backroom, and stepping briskly towards me, declares, "Shouldn't do that, you know. Need to give it to the people who work here; more theirs than yours, don't you think?"

Although it is a calm balloon face, nothing sneerful, even smiling, as if lost money and happiness go together, I respond in an anger that is only half real. "Not theirs either."

This new backroom Diner man answers, "But they are closer to the owner than you are; hence, logically, only right you hand it over to them. Only right."

It's the hence part that I find extra bothersome, and so, "Finders keepers, losers…."

"But it's their place. Their Diner, in a sense it's their house, see what I mean? Their house. It's only right."

"And that someone, that theirs, wouldn't happen to be you, would it?"

"Doesn't have to be me. Even though, now, I am the only one here," motioning to show me empty chairs and tables. "Only me."

"Where is Charles?"

"Later, he'll be in later of course. If you wish I can give the money to him. As you wish."

"You're serious?"

"Absolutely."

I am speechless and can't imagine how he saw me pick up the money from the backroom, behind closed doors, this early in the morning. We both stop to survey the Diner floor, as if there might be more money lying about ownerless.

4

Later, as I think about leaving campus early simply because I want to, Laura, piano teacher *extraordinaire,* leans in. "Hi."

"Hi yourself."

Laura is new and too serious to teach piano to students who see it as nothing more than an after-dinner hobby. Piano has been her life since she was five, since Taiwan, NYC, Washington DC—her life. She is almost famous in the world of classical pianists and has no business teaching here, in the desert, on the Gulf, with students who once petitioned the president to make Shishah 101 a real course.

"How goes it?"

"It goes."

"Any academic silliness to share?"

Because Laura is reed thin and Chinese, her age remains a mystery.

"Nothing really. Same silliness, different players."

"Aha, well then listen to this," moving closer to find a better storytelling position. "Student goes to teacher and says, 'I don't need to practice the piano because I'm pretty good at it already.'

Student stops to let that sink in before continuing: 'Which probably means I will get an A for the class without even trying, *sah*—without even trying.'" She hesitates to let the student take a breath, smile, maybe even give her a wink. Laura sits down. "As of today, right now," pushing my papers aside, her piano-playing fingertips running back and forth across the desktop, "as of this moment he is, at best, … at best, … an average student piano player: but forget all that because he is coming to argue with me about this, and I can hardly wait. The boy who need not practice, who believes the piano is a toy to tinker with—*SAH?*" Pulling her hands back, off the table and into her lap, smiling a smile that come to think of it may not be a smile at all.

"Let me know how that turns out." And with that the telephone rings and Laura, with smile, disappears out the office door.

The verdict to John's grade appeal is overdue. This is not a good sign for John—policy squabbles within the committee. Then there is Peter and his Milton project. I secretly worry about him, after all these years, his project coming to fruition. This is both good and bad—good in that it is finally finished, complete, bad in that it will leave a hole in his academic universe. A new project will have to be invented. Until then, Peter's life will be meaningless.

I catch a glimpse of Sara just before she slips into her office. It is hard to tell with Sara but there is a hint of redness around her eyes and neck that is either a sign of anger or sadness, sometimes both. I linger at her office door, reading her office hours, along with a shopping list of foolishly wise quotes from famous writers about learning, education, life. I read until I am rescued by a student who boldly taps on her office door. She answers with a firm "No." The student— cheeky pimples with something like an idea of a beard—looks at me, and I offer a shrug. I can see he is thinking about knocking again and I suggest, "If I were you, I would wait until the coast is clear—if I were you." I don't know if he understands what I mean, but he turns and walks away like he does.

As I am leaving the bathroom, white-chef-hat Charles is entering. We say hello, and I ask what he is doing way up here in the rarified ether of the fifth floor. He simply gives his head a shake, saying, "Yeah, how about that."

But then, "By the way, your new backroom man seems over-ly-concerned about money. What's that about?"

"What?"

"The new guy you hired for the backroom, the one who gave me a thorough reprimand for pocketing 250 *fils* from your diner floor. In essence, he said it was more his than mine. Quite an addition you got there, Charles."

"Dr. Martin, I have no idea what you're talking about. I haven't hired anybody new, not a soul. Who's got the budget for more people? You? Sorry, Doc, now if you'll excuse me," and he left abruptly.

❧❧❧

I end up staring at her sandals, her toenails painted a bright orange, but there's more: they are long toes with the burnt orange making them larger, longer, bordering on freakish. She explains that it is not her fault, but her father's, that "... he insisted I drive him to the airport, park the car, walk with him to the departure gate, give him a hug and tell him I will miss him, and only then was I free to go, and by then I had already missed Dr. Ahmad's class." And so, "You can see how my absence has nothing to do with me, not really. My father's the one. He says family is more important than anything else. Says family is what we are all about, not university or grades or some smartypants professor who believes 'To be or not to be' will make a difference." Stopping here because she is out of breath.

"Your father said all of that?"

"Well, ..." wiggling her toes, "well, yes, most of it."

She and her toenails have made me weary and now that she has run out of breath, I tell her, "Don't worry, I will speak to Professor Ahmad for you. Things can be worked out, I am sure."

But her look tells me it won't be that easy, frowning down at her sandals. I try again. "Listen, I am the chair of the department and I will speak to Dr. Ahmad about your situation. All's well that ends well. Believe me."

This seems to help. "Ok, ok. But remember, it's my father's fault. Professor Ahmad thinks absences are terrible; he says punctuality is the key to responsibility. Trust is all about being on time, proving one's worth. This is what he says."

I am mildly surprised; I had no idea Ahmad thought this way, and when I smirk, she questions. "That's funny?"

"No, no, not you. Of course not. But you believe Professor

Ahmad to be right on this, about punctuality and responsibility? You believe this?"

This, I can tell, was not part of the script she practiced. She waits and considers. "Yes, I can say yes. He is the professor after all, so yes. I have to believe him."

Once she leaves, I turn to send Ahmad an email, but when I do I realize I don't know her name, the class, even when she was absent. I write: "Ahmad, if any girls were absent recently from any of your classes, I am sure they had good reason."

The class hasn't even started, and already students are glancing at their wristwatches, turning to look out the window, staring over my shoulder, at the blank wall, at the blanker whiteboard. Sabika, who sits in the front, who is not afraid to wear dresses, whose knees always seem to shine, to glisten, smiles, nods and writes something in her notebook. I can't imagine I have said anything worth writing down, and I step closer to see. A heavy fluttering interrupts. Someone in the corner has dropped a book, papers—a boy whose name I am still not sure about, who's trying to grow a moustache, sideburns. Before I can step his direction, the book and papers are neatly back on the desk, and he, too, looks up, smiles and nods.

In the end, I ask if there are any questions. The wind is blowing, the dust moving in fog-like. I have gone overtime, and economic students are at the door, daring to be shooed away. Heading back to my office, a boy catches up with me, asking, "Will you be in your office today?" He is carrying three thick books. There is nothing familiar about him; his face is new. "It's important," smiling, as if importance and smiling go together.

I look harder, longer at him—a girlish straight-back gloss to his hair, a nose that might have been broken once. *Boys carrying around thick books. What's that about?* I find myself saying, "Why would I want to go to my office?"

He doesn't move, blinking, waiting for what has to be more, something else. Finally, his smile lingering, as if it has nowhere else to go, he says, "Yes, why would you."

As I watch him go, I do three things: close my eyes, sigh, and do something that can only be called a grinding of teeth.

That night I dream that someone is knocking at the front door. I struggle to reach the door but there are obstacles everywhere: the twelve-year-old wants her bicycle fixed, my wife wants me to read this, listen to that, students suddenly appear to tap me on the shoulder, insisting that they have to meet with me, if not now when—it's important. But a pounding at the door, demanding to be let in right this minute. "You hear me? Right now."

The next day, around noon, the day is humid, wet and jungle sticky, and as I pass by Sara's office she is standing there as if it isn't her office at all; she sees me and says, "Come here." And I do. "Sit down." I start to do that too when she says, "No, I didn't mean it. Don't sit."

"What?"

"You know, not only is she smart but she's intelligent, too.

These are two completely different ideas, you know—smart and intelligent. People believe they are the same but they are not. But never mind, I am a professional educator, and some people may not like me, even hate me, but I really don't care. Why should I? Regardless, I am always ready to do my part, more than my part, and when I asked her what she plans to do after graduation, I wanted to hear the words graduate school, I wanted to hear something about graduate studies, about going above and beyond all of this." She motions toward the door, the hallway and beyond. "Of all the students I wanted to hear that most of all from Dana." She struggles to stop, to take a breath, looking down at her palms as if she knows something about fortune-telling. We wait until finally, as I ready myself to slide back into the hallway, she rubs her cheek, saying, "But what does she say? Dana, how does she respond?" I think, what did Dana tell me with that girlie grin on her face? What? I remember and I recite it slowly to Dana.

"I plan to marry, he is waiting for me to finish; I want to have children, two, maybe three', giggling, 'and then, follow my husband where ever he decides because he's an engineer, or will be soon, you know and has family in Cairo. Of course I will do whatever he believes is right for me, for us'."

Sara and I return to silence. I can hear the rooster in the backyard across the street.

"You understand," she says, reaching out to take hold of my sleeve, "Dana is absolutely the very best I have, have had for quite a while. You understand that?"

I know Dana is highly intelligent, but I answer with, "She is?"

"Of course," Sara says, giving my sleeve a yank.

I continue to stand at her desk, and even think of sitting down but instead say, noncommittally, "I see."

That is when she stops to stare, and with a smirk, announces, "You have no idea what I am talking about. Do you?"

"No, I do, I do." And for the first time in a very long time I mean it with Sara.

"It's Dana Mohammed, you know her. We all know her, right?"

"Yes…yes." For some strange reason I am annoyed that she thinks I don't know who she is talking about, and that some of her anger is moving in my direction.

"Dana, an outstanding student in every way," Sara says with a frown. "She is, as they say, the real deal." She drops my sleeve and moves to her chair behind her desk and sits. She moves a stack of papers from left to right and then back again.

"And?"

"And, aren't you listening? What good are you? I just spoke with her and she's graduating and when I asked her what was next, after graduation, what's next? Come to think of it I even said graduate school. Made it into a real question, graduate school? And you know what she said?"

"Yes, I think I got that part."

No longer caring about me, "She wants marriage and children and what? Staying at home to watch TV? Go shopping? Are you listening to me, to her? All that energy and intelligence and clear writing, all those good ideas, and for what; to tell me that it's all about marriage and kids and doing her husband's will? What's that? Worst of all, she tells me all this with a smile. Imagine? A smile. This is ok for the rest of them, not a bad idea, and good luck, but not Dana. Even you see that, right?"

I start to say something wise and department-chair-like, "Well…"

"Well hell." And the tears come. "You just don't get it do you: students like Dana Mohammad are what I'm all about. Without her and what she can do, her potential, . . ," wiggling her fingers. "It's what I'm all about."

I offer a mild, "Maybe she will change her mind if she hears your speech."

She snorts.

"Your speech."

Sara angrily wipes away the tears as if they have no business being there, saying, "Right, speech. I think I am done for the day. Good-bye," ending with a scowl, and "Shut the door on your way out."

Once in the hallway, like some late-night lover slipping out before sunrise, I look both ways to see who might have seen or heard.

∞∞∞

Jaffar is our house man, *haris*, who stops by every morning to wash the car, to pick up stray garbage, to water the flowers and maybe, if he is in the mood, to even coil the green hose—and feed the dog, if it will let him. Jaffar is from Cairo, we think, but even if he isn't it doesn't matter. We pay him ten dinar every week, even if he doesn't feed the dog, or coil the hose. This, we know, is too much money, and in his own-Egyptian way, Jaffar knows it too. It is not something to discuss—just slipping the money into his hand every Thursday morning—*Shukran*. Most of the morning Jaffar will sit on his stool in front of the house and have tea and smoke cigarettes with the neighbor's *haris*, Jacob, who, I am certain, is Indian, somewhere near Goa. I sometimes watch them from my second-floor study and wonder what they can be sitting and talking about for so long: the heat, the sand, terrorism, how much money they send home to their families, or not? No matter what, there is much laughter, the constant puffing of cigarettes, fingering their *misbahas*. Jaffar has the complexion of dark well-polished mahogany, and when I try to imagine a younger Jaffar, in Cairo—or maybe Luxor—going to school, playing with other children, I only see a smaller older Jaffar, with cigarette neatly leaning from his boyish mouth. Sometimes Jaffar and Jacob will catch me looking down at them and when they do, they wave, laugh and wave some more like they are on holiday. I am sure there is an Arab saying for this laughing at someone who is watching them and then waving at the watcher, but I can't imagine what it might be.

Jaffar is missing an important front tooth, but never mind because as if by design, everything works out: his cigarettes fitting perfectly into that toothy blankness. Waving some more, flicking ashes here and there until Jacob has to remind him that the ash is flying his way, be careful, and of course this is funny too. Jaffar is good at talking to the boys who often walk by the house, making their way from the elementary school at the end of the street. He seems to have long, heart-felt questions to ask, while they answer with a *nam* or *lah, lah* or silence. If he sees the boys smoking, he will get extra loud, even shout at them as they scurry past. Jacob thinks this is funny. Jacob tells me Jaffar hates seeing boys smoke because they don't know what they're doing. *These know nothing boys.* The boys pay him little mind, walking faster and maybe even flicking a lit cigarette his direction.

The next morning I come to the office later than usual just to see what it feels like, and just when I am liking it just fine, there is a knock at the door and in walks a bright white, squareish *dishdasha.*

"Sorry to bother you, professor, but there is a problem."

"There is?"

"My son Hamad tells me there is a problem?"

"There is?"

"Yes? Sad to say, a big problem."

"Please, sit down and tell me," I say, opening my hands wide to show I am ready to be told.

"Yes, thank you," and folding his *dishdasha* just right, he slowly lowers himself onto the very edge of the chair, as if there is no need to use the entire chair, taking up all its shiny black plastic because he isn't staying long. He begins, "Professor, do you know the Arabic word *ehteram?*"

"No, I am afraid I don't, what does it mean?"

"It is a very important word in our culture."

"Yes, and what does it mean?"

"This word means everything to us," placing one hand on his chest to show me where the 'everything' lives, while motioning towards the window with the other to show me that the 'us' is out there, beyond the window.

I nod to this, and when I do, like a kind of signal a pigeon floats out of the sky to land neatly on the window ledge. When I turn to see, another pigeon follows. I continue to nod as the two pigeons watch one another, and then me, and now one another, and . . .

"It means respect."

I lean back in my chair, steeple my fingers together under my chin, and shut my eyes, whispering, "Ah". I know what will follow; I've heard it before, from students, parents, cousins, brothers, assorted sisters and uncles. *Ehteram.*

"Yes, well, before we continue, perhaps, I need to speak to your son, Hamad. Is he here?"

"Here? Today? No, he is home. Have you seen the dust and wind today, and they say it will continue until Wednesday. So, no, he is home in bed. The day is terrible."

"I see. I wasn't aware there was a problem about respect," I say, talking straight into my steepled fingers.

Only now does the father, who hasn't stopped sitting on the chair's edge, remove his sunglasses, placing them carefully on the desktop. "But it is very simple, no need for my son to be here to tell you what he has already told me."

I wait, and the pigeons, tired of watching, flutter away.

"Yes, you yelled at him. In class, in front of his classmates, his friends, you yelled at him. This is unacceptable. This is disrespect-ful. You can see that? Be it professors, students, it does not matter. Respect is for all to enjoy."

I turn ever so slightly to stare out the window. The father is not wrong: it is another dusty day that has no sun, a vast yellow-ness filling the sky.

"Respect."

"Yes," says the father, as if finally we are getting somewhere.

"Mr. Saeed, your son Hamad has a temper. Did you know that?"

'Of course," turning his palms up, as if 'of course' were some-thing to hold. "We all do. Sad to say, this is human nature."

"No, Mr. Saeed, your son has a temper, and sometimes, in fact, often, he does not know how to control it. But surely you know this. As his father you know this."

"What is this temper?" All done with the 'of course', he uses both hands to mix the air in front of him. "It's everywhere. We are men, and men are this way. A man without temper is not a man. Everybody knows this."

Like a kind of magic, Mr. Saeed suddenly is holding a ciga-rette, gently rolling it between his fingertips. His eyebrows are a strange swatch of blackbrownred, as if somewhere, at some time, someone couldn't make up his mind.

"But never mind, because it all comes back to you because you are in charge, you are the model," announces Mr. Saeed with a smile. "As teacher, professor, you are always the role model, and my son—all of them—are watching you to see how to act, how to behave. This, too, is your job, Professor. Yes, your job."

By now my steepled fingers have collapsed, and I, leaning over the desk, say, "Yes, but respect runs two ways, and when he throws a pencil in the classroom, at the wall, this is disrespectful towards me, the class."

"Ah, that is nothing. He is yet a boy, and boys do this. Sad but true."

"Mr. Saeed, Hamad is what? Twenty, twenty-one years old?"

He stops rolling the cigarette between his fingertips to ask, "He threw a pencil?" His eyebrows meeting in the middle.

"He didn't tell you this part?"

"Still, you yelled at him in front of his friends, his classmates. This is not right."

This is when a beeping comes from Mr. Saeed's pocket. It beeps three, four times until finally I say, "Maybe you should answer that."

Mr. Saeed pulls out the small machine that is beeping, pokes at it with a finger and places it back in his pocket, announcing, "No, it is nothing."

It beeps three more times before stopping.

Finally, Mr. Saeed can wait no longer, and holding up the cigarette for all to see, asks, "May I smoke?"

"No, smoking is not allowed in the building."

"*Akeed,*" he answers, and returns to rolling the cigarette harder, faster between his fingertips. "So I think we can agree that what happened was wrong, disrespectful, and as you know the best way to solve things like this is to apologize. It has come to this—an apology."

I offer him a smile, and after waiting for a small silence to fill, watching him finger his cigarette, moving his sunglasses across the table, from there to here, say, "Yes, I agree, and I will gladly accept Hamad's apology. Class is tomorrow. I look forward to his apology, the entire class does."

"*Lah,*" but even Hamad's father can only take so much, enough is enough, and slips the cigarette in his mouth. "You have it all wrong. Of course the apology must come from you. You yelled at him in front of his friends, his classmates. We have already established that this is disrespectful. Please do your duty."

"Yes, but what's to be done with the pencil throwing part? What's to be done?"

Mr. Saeed, his sitting on the edge of the black chair all finished, does four things, almost all at the same time: he picks up his sunglasses, puts them on his face, stands and announces, "I think we are done here."

When I stand, Mr. Saeed's machine starts beeping again, and this time he answers. With cigarette in mouth, sunglasses firmly on face, the small machine pressed tight against his ear, Mr. Saeed smiles. The issue of respect, of *ehteram,* has been dealt with, made clear, demands have been made, and now, he can leave, convinced he has done his fatherly duty, and then some.

ঔঔঔ

The grade appeals committee has ruled and Maryam's petition is denied. A 48% final grade cannot be ignored. I await John's telephone call, or at the very least an official memo, but as the afternoon wears on there is nothing. This is both good and bad. In fact, the entire morning has been a pleasant surprise: no one of consequence at my door, dreary uneventful emails. I check my calendar: no meetings scheduled, office hour from 1-2, with rest of the afternoon yawning out into an academic desert. But not so fast, ... There is talk that an ambulance has arrived on campus, near the administration building; and sure enough when I go to the window, there it is, neatly tucked in the no parking zone, green lights flashing. I wait for activity. I think of heart attacks, falling downstairs, heat exhaustion. Finally, done waiting, I return to my desk. Two military helicopters hover along the beachfront.

Nasreen is waiting for me when I walk into class early, and although she says good morning, I can tell it's the fluff of unimportant talk. What she really means is that she can't read my writing, holding up her paper alongside her head. I put down my briefcase and say good morning back, but she is not looking at me, only her paper. I squint at the pages, following the aim of her finger as she asks, "And what is this?"

"'Very', the word is 'very,'" I answer.

She looks closer at the very. By now I know Nasreen, and she cares nothing about the word very; I wait for the other, the rest, the bigger, more important questions. Finally, "This grade is no good."

Together, we look at the letter D she is pointing to.

"Yes, you're right."

Her finger refuses to leave the paper, the D. "This is not right."

I wait.

"I mean, this grade is not right."

Still, waiting, watching her finger, her well-chewed fingernails.

"You grade too hard."

"Think so?"

"Of course. Everybody says so. So hard, so unfair."

By now others have started to come in, sitting here, standing there, making that last- minute cellphone call because for the next fifty minutes they will be out of touch.

"For example?"

She sighs, letting me know she cares nothing for examples. "For example, here. What is this?"

"That's what we call a run-on sentence. You may recall we talked about that last week, and the week before that, and . . ."

"Ok, it's a run-on sentence, but you can still understand my feelings, my words, can't you?"

"Yes, I can."

"Then what's so bad? Understanding is most important, right?"

"Yes, that's part of it."

My yes seems to help and she edges closer, her shoulder brushing mine, her hair leaning across my arm. More students fill the room. Some of them have decided to listen, as if my answers may in some way be of use to them later on.

"Nasreen, class is about to begin. We'll talk more after class."

She pulls her finger away from the run-on sentence.

Nasreen has new jewelry, rings on her thumbs, one, a kind of wrap-a-round silver, the other a glistening gold.

For the first time, Nasreen does not linger after class; she does not stop to dig through her bag to find that elusive something; she does not wave good-bye at the door. She leaves with the others.

5

Sara is still in mourning over Dana Mohammad, and when we share the elevator, she seems mesmerized by the gray elevator door, staring straight ahead. She exits with a "Good talking to you."

Marshall comes up behind me in the hallway, and placing his hand on my shoulder, whispers, "They are at it again."

"Hello, Marshall."

His hand staying on my shoulder. "Did you hear what I said: they are at it again."

I wait for him to tell me more, but Marshall is not like that, smiling, waiting, hand a little tighter on my shoulder, until I sigh, "What do you mean?"

Now he can drop his hand. "There is rumor of recall, of recalling you as chair. Like that time two years ago, only now, bigger. Right?"

We move to the side to let two students amble by.

"Only rumor?"

He shrugs, "Rumor, but I must say it carries a grain of truth, you see."

He is enjoying this, and I indulge him. "Who's the culprit this time, the unhappy party?"

"Rumor has it that it's Thomas."

"Thomas?" I am genuinely surprised, and Marshall is beside himself with glee.

"But I almost never ever see the man, none of us do."

"Ah, and there you have it."

Thomas Chapel is the ghost of the department. He specializes in teaching evening classes, holds office hours in the middle of the night and can almost never find the time or energy to attend meetings. When I do chance to catch him in his office, he almost always has a student sitting in front of him, and when I offer a friendly department-chair wave, he stares at me in what can only be measured as disbelief. His office door reads: Professor of Rhetoric and Composition. There are no clever cartoons, no witty sayings. Below his title he has scribbled: Office hours: 8:00pm-9:30pm, MW. Because one of Thomas's nostrils is larger, darker than the other, whenever I do chance to see him, maybe even speak to him, I can't help but talk to his nose.

"Thomas? Well, and what does he say?"

"The rumor says that he says you don't support him, have never supported him."

"Support?"

"Says the rumor."

More students shuffle by. "Good morning, professors." I wait until they disappear around the corner.

"You're kidding?"

Marshall, his job done, reattaches his hand to my shoulder before announcing, "Bye, bye." And strolls away.

℞℞℞

When I walk out into the garden that is more pebbles and sand than flowers and grass, the dog looks up at me, whimpering because he wants to play, be fed, both, but sitting loyally at my feet looking up. I don't look down at him, but with arms folded I study the way the clouds are mushroom rosy. For what feels like a long time, I stand in the garden with dog and think of things like sentence fragments, thesis statements, comma splices and D papers. All of this moves smoothly between a brightening sky and a moaning dog.

The next day the wind and dust are brutal; paper and plastic bags twisting and swirling, dust devils racing through intersections. People are pushed and pulled as they cross the street, and when they finally get to a door, they are gritty, hair-funny and angry. Because of the dust and wind—the red-eyed sun—parents will insist their sons and daughters stay home because too many unpleasant things can happen on days like this. Plastic bags grabbing at your legs like worried children, students and staff stumbling through the gates, a palm frond cartwheeling down the middle of the street. Looking Gulf-ward, there is a roil of brown and gray on the horizon, of watercolors gone bad.

Ros calls, asking, "How are you?" but before I can answer she continues, "Fine, hey listen, I need to talk with you. It's urgent."

After nine years I know exactly what her urgent means. It

means not urgent, in fact nothing even close to urgent. More like something along the lines of a topic of interest. As she waits for me to respond, I lie and tell her I am speaking with a student now but will stop by when I am done, and by the way, "What's so urgent?"

I ask this already knowing the answer. "I'll tell you when you stop by."

I trump her urgent with an "Okiedokie."

My door is shut, locked, and from 10:00 to 10:30 there are three knocks, two knocks accompanied by strong doorknob twisting. I get up to check the hallway window, adjusting the blinds to make sure there are no gaps, no slivers of openness where people can peer in.

Finally, my talking with no student all done, I aim for her office, and as expected the urgency is, "Would you be willing to chair the Promotions Committee?"

This is not urgent but I rub my chin and forehead like it is, and as she waits for my answer, I ask, "Who else is on the committee?"

"Wilson in Math, Dr. Suliman in Biology, Martinez in Spanish, and you, if you accept."

"Get rid of Wilson and I'll think about it."

"Why's that?"

"His arrogance is overwhelming, his sense of righteousness Neanderthal. Besides, half the time he never shows for meetings but you can damn well expect him to place the committee work on his end of year evaluation. Get rid of Wilson, and the answer is yes."

She does not like the Neanderthal part but I can tell she agrees with the other.

"Anything else?" I ask.

"No, I think that's it for the time being, unless…" and she lingers to scratch one eyebrow, then the other, her scratching continuing until, "Unless you would like to revisit the Marshall issue."

"The Marshall issue?" I question, which it really isn't because I know precisely where this is going.

"Yes, the Marshall question."

I can't pretend anymore. "Oh, that."

"Yes, you know we really must get rid of him. The students are afraid of him, he is rude and calls it individualism. We cannot get enough students to take his classes, even if they are core classes. They would rather wait and graduate late than take a class with him, Dr. Monster Marshall, if I may quote one disgruntled student. This is not good."

"Yes, I remember now."

'It is my husband.' Holding up her cellphone for all to see. 'I must take this call. My husband.'

'I don't give a good God damn who it is.'

A chunk of silence, followed by somebody's too loud radio from the street. The rooster answers. I can visualize it now: John rubbing his hands together because he thinks he's made his point abundantly clear, while heads look down at their notes, or maybe rereading the many confessionals scratched into the desktops. Once the silence is all used up, she, with cellphone tightly clutched, stalks out of the classroom, slamming the door behind her.

Later, I will hear different versions of what happened: one from the student/wife, one from John and others from assorted students who were there, saw, heard all, even, at the very end, a telephone call from the furious husband himself. Like always, all versions are right, all wrong, and I have to decide where the best truth is.

੿੿੿

Outside the Diner, Dean Ros and the president are deep in what can only be described as administrative conversation, as they lean into one another, arms folded, turning this way and that. I emerge from the elevator with nothing in my hands, no newspaper, no student papers, no registration forms, nothing to look down at, to stare into, and so when I look their way, they too cannot pretend not to see me, and the president, unfolding his arms, motions me over. I quickly hold up a hand and point at my wristwatch. Both he and Ros seem satisfied with this, the president excusing me with a return nod that says 'yes, of course you have class,' or 'yes, some other time' or 'yes, good idea, I'm in no mood to talk with you either;' all of which means I have to step back into the elevator I just stepped out of and retreat to the fifth-floor office I just left.

As I reenter my office, wondering how long I might have to wait before the coast is clear, I hear sirens, and almost immediately Nepalese security is at the door, cellphone in hand, out of breath, glistening with sweat, imploring that I, "Please leave."

"What?'

"Please leave."

"Why?"

"There is a bomb."

"There is?" I quickly go to the window and scan the campus, as if I look long and hard enough, I might be able to spy what the stuff of bomb looks like: a brown paper bag propped up against a bench, with a tangle of wires bristling out of it, or maybe some schoolish backpack innocently leaning against the front door of the library. Instead, there is only a herd of students strolling leisurely towards the parking lot.

The security man is waiting for me, and I turn and ask, "Anything else?"

He can only stare.

"Ok, I'm going."

Bomb scares like these not only send us scurrying to the parking lot, but also give us a chance to visit faculty and staff that we haven't seen for semesters, even years. Coffee cups in hand while bags of potato chips are passed around, we catch up on gossip and hearsay: undeserving, thankless students, wayward administrators, our never-enough salaries. By now black cars with sirens have arrived and uniformed men with weapons and dogs hop out and begin their campus search. I see a dean who I thought retired, a student who should have graduated two years ago, faces that look familiar smile and wave in my direction. Meanwhile, the Nepalese security force roams the now-shut gates. Cellphones at the ready. Their shirts stained black with sweat.

In another thirty minutes, the emergency will be over and the all-clear signal given. Later, at the dinner table, if asked by Mom and Dad what happened at school today: 'Anything interesting? What did you learn?' students will calmly answer nothing, and go back to their cellphones with fried chicken.

The next morning, for the first time in a long time, I decide on a taxi. Like always, their honking lets you know they're there, or almost there, but right behind you, if you're interested, and this shouldn't surprise me but it does and I can't help but give a small, startled twitch before raising my hand like some school boy; and sure enough a taxi slides up next to me, stopping where it shouldn't but never mind because although he started it, I did raise my hand, so that's that.

This taxi has nothing like automatic windows so I have to open the door to talk with him. He sits mildly, not even bothering to glance my way, as if driving a taxi is not his idea.

"I am going to Salmiya," I announce.

Only now does he turn to look at me, not even a real look, more like an annoying glimpse, before saying, "I am not going that way.'

I nod, followed by a small wait before asking, "You are a taxi, right?"

"Most assuredly," he says, sounding like something he once read.

"I need to go to Salmiya," I try again.

"Yes, I am not going that way," he sighs, shifting in the seat. I wait, door wide open and he waits, shifting again, until "It's too far and almost impossible to find anyone who wants a taxi there. They're all Pakistanis, mobs of Egyptians, and who knows what else but none of them are looking for a taxi, and then there's always the teenagers who need a ride to school, to the mall, to the shisha café, who never pay, who jump out at the stop light and run away, laughing, thinking it's all great fun that they have taken up my time and gasoline. So, no, I am not headed to Salmiya. How about some place else? Salwa is a nice neighborhood. Salwa?"

'No, Salmiya is for me."

"Ok, listen," he says, talking to his hands that have a firm grip on the steering wheel. "Three dinar, and I'll think about it. Three dinar."

"How about two? Two is more realistic."

"You are not serious. Two dinar is nothing."

More honking behind us as another taxi cruises by. By now he is frowning into his mirror. I watch him look for something in his shirt pocket that is not there, can't be found and he returns to frowning into the mirror. Now, out of nowhere, a radio is playing, and we both lift our heads to listen. His arms are strangely hairy, even curliques here and there, and for some reason I think this funny, turning my head to read a sticker on the windshield that tells me that God loves me—always has, always will.

"But you want to make money. I mean, that is what a taxi does, takes people from here to there, and you make money."

"Yes, again, the taking you there is the easy part but the returning empty, with nobody paying, is the hard part. Besides, the traffic is terrible this time of day, you know that. Take a look," he says, motioning with his chin.

And when I do, it looks like normal traffic to me. I shrug.

"Too bad you couldn't come earlier or later, but now, with this traffic, it will be impossible, especially if you're in a hurry."

"I am in no hurry."

"Ah, that's what they all say." By now he has taken one hand off the steering wheel, letting it rest on the eyeless meter that looks old or broken, or both.

"I'm going to work," I say suddenly, feeling the urge to explain myself, as if in some special taxicab way that will make a difference.

Now it is his turn to shrug.

All the while leaning across his front seat, I see his floor is littered with cigarette butts, gum waiting to be chewed, or not, and dangling from his rearview mirror is one of those many-armed Hindu goddesses, ruby lips, an indifferent gaze. And that is when I see the comb—a red comb. It is there, among the tissues, used or not, along with assorted peanuts. I look at him, the comb, him, the comb. He is bald, this taxi driver. Oh, there is a rim of fuzz around his ears but aside from that nothing but a dimpled blankness.

Thinking by now that enough is enough and that there are other taxis to be had, maybe too many, I step back onto the curb, and just before I shut his door—thinking that giving it a good slam would not be a bad idea—he, back to staring straight ahead, says what sounds like a question, "two and a half dinar?"

I want to ask him about the red comb. For two and a half

dinar he will owe me an explanation. Still, I nod a nod that is designed to be neither yes nor no. There is more deep sighing from him that says he hasn't got all day. The radio has stopped as another taxi goes by, and then another. This one flashing its lights. All of this is more to frown about. As I ready to shut the door again, thinking more about hair than taxis, I hear, "Fine, two dinar."

I slide into the backseat.

Two stoplights later...

His head hits the windshield with a watermelon-thud, followed by a frantic spiderwebbing of glass. The taxi driver screeches to a halt and jumps out yelling at the hit man, who does his best to scream back but on second thought crumbles to the side of the road.

From the backseat I see it all; the way he decides to swerve around the stopped bus, the way the green-shirted man is suddenly right there, in the middle of the road, imagining all he must do is scurry and all will be well. But now the green-shirted man is turning pale and silent, sliding down next to a row of recently trimmed roadside bushes; and although the taxi driver is still yelling, the green-shirted man, like a sleeper, stretches out in the dirt and pebbles. Only then does the driver stop. Suddenly, the police, like a kind of magic, are there, lights flashing, demanding IDs and licenses, along with some mild pushing, a finger in the face. The man on the ground does not say a word but with eyes wide open a bright redness crawls across his forehead. Wait for the police to ask me questions: *Did you see? What happened? Who are you?* But nothing; I am just another backseat customer. That is when I open the door, step into the street lined with cars that have stopped, slowed, wanting to see, and do two things: I look at my watch and see that I am late and reach into my pocket and hand the driver two KD. He looks at the money, then at me, and then back to the police who are only getting louder, the squawk of their radios. I can walk the rest of the way. Looking back, I see a policeman now bending over the green-shirted man, urging him to stand up. "That's enough, enough. *Kafa, kafa.*" All the while, one of his sandals leisurely sits in the middle of the street, as if on display. I am late and wonder if they will start the meeting without me.

That night, the younger one, as if our roles were suddenly reversed, asks, "How was your day, Daddy?"

I think about this for a moment, because, as a rule, nobody ever asks me that, and I genuinely must think back over the day, until, sounding like her, like all of them, say, "Ok, it was ok. And you?"

But she is not to be deterred, and repeats, "Ok, but what happened today, Daddy? What happened with you today?"

"Nothing."

She tilts her head birdlike, eyeing me. "Really? Nothing at all?"

Forced to remember, I say, "Well, there was something, but really it is nothing."

"Tell me, Daddy. Tell me about this something that is nothing."

This is when I look at her more closely and wonder if this is a trap—her mother's doing. And so, taking a deep breath, I tell her all about how the taxi driver hit the green-shirted man walking across the street. It is not the full telling, and I leave out many details, but it doesn't matter.

"Really? You saw a murder?" Her eyes growing wide.

"Well, no, I wouldn't call it that. He was on the ground, bleeding, but I don't know about the murder part."

"Daddy, you saw a murder."

"No, not exactly."

But by now there is no stopping her, and she springs out of the room, yelling for all to hear, "Daddy saw a murder. Everybody, Daddy saw a murder."

The rest of the evening turns into a complicated retelling of the morning's drama: the way the driver swerved around the bus and there he was, head meets windshield, then the driver with grounded green-shirted man and assorted police all playing out their parts. Once I finish and it is bedtime and I don't remember having done so much talking at one sitting, she disappointingly murmurs, "So it wasn't a murder? You didn't see a murder?"

I let the question linger, before, "Like I said, the policeman was urging him to get up. Does that sound like a murder to you?"

Meanwhile, the others having already announced, 'Yep, that's something all right' have moved off into other rooms, leaving only this one.

"No, I guess not."

"So, there you have it."

"There you have it."

As she walks wilted toward the door, in a burst of fatherly guilt, I say, "But if he did die, you're right, it would be a kind of murder—if he did die."

This stops her, and with something like a well-worn smile she whispers, "I knew it."

ب‎ ب‎ ب‎

In front and to the right of the lovers sits Bedour. When called upon she painfully squeezes out the biggest, best answers. Bedour has never once felt the need to raise her hand. I must wait for her to lift her eyes from the book, the desktop before, "And Bedour, what do you think?" I know all about Bedour: high school teachers have told her that her writing is wonderful, unique, correct, that she has a way with words, and, oh, by the way, has she ever thought about going into journalism? So yes, I know Bedour. She doesn't watch TV, but reads; in fact, reading is like a drug to her and without her daily read she feels terrible, rotten, her day is ruined. Why go out with friends when she can stay home and read about love and death and hate and more love. Anything less than a grade of A and she pouts.

Nasreen has cut her hair. That, and she no longer sits up front but has taken a seat in the back, two seats from Yousef. When Yousef leans to say something to her, she nods, smiles and touches the tips of her new hair.

I talk about the research paper, due in two weeks, and almost immediately Yousef raises his hand, asking, "Why?"

"Why?"

"Yeah, why do we have to do a research paper?" Folding his arms across his chest. "I mean, how useful will writing a research paper ever be for us, any of us? I mean, really?"

I shrug.

Even the lovers take time out to listen, looking first at Yousef, then me, now back to Yousef. Nasreen hasn't stopped fingering her new hair.

I ready myself to say something long, complicated and professorial, but then, at the last moment, change my mind and say, "It will be good for you."

Bedour looks straight at me. The lovers twitter.

"That's it?" says Yousef.

"That's it."

I can tell that Yousef is disappointed and was hoping for more of a verbal brawl. Bedour goes back to looking down at her desktop; the lovers go back to each other. Somebody somewhere snickers. Nasreen is looking at Yousef.

If there is a contest in any of this, a sense of winners and losers, Yousef is winning but strangely I feel nothing like defeat.

Mohammed comes to me after class, asking if there is anything he can do.

"Do?"

"Yes, to improve my grade?"

"You're not doing well?"

"I am failing, professor."

Of course I know Mohammad is failing, and has been for many weeks now, and yet, . . . "Really?"

"Yes, really."

The silence of a classroom on a Thursday afternoon, after research-paper talk. Moving a stack of papers from here to there, slipping a book into my briefcase, I look into Mohammed's face, a face that doesn't want to look back, that almost certainly would rather be looking anywhere else but at me.

"If I don't pass my dad will be furious."

This is the longest, most complicated sentence Mohammed has ever spoken to me.

"I see."

"You know how it is."

"How's that?"

"It's an Arabic thing, this good grade stuff."

More nodding.

"Is there something I can do, like extra credit?"

"Extra credit?"

"Sure, something like that." Looking down at his shoes and then at the green hospital-like wall as if there is something important there.

"I don't have anything like that."

Mohammad slanting in front of me, saying nothing and then nodding as if he has heard wisdom.

⋙⋘

The day is about done when I look up and Ahmad has stepped into my office. Not surprisingly he is holding his mandatory stack of student papers, but there is something else, something more, his moustache hangs weakly, drained of all moustache energy.

"Martin, sorry to bother you but I have an issue; we can even call it an emergency of sorts. Well, . ." shifting his papers to the other hand, "Well, if not an emergency, then something close to it."

There is that small gap of indecisiveness as to who will go next, until finally I say, "Tell me."

"Yes, well, sad to say, the doctor tells me I need surgery."

"He did and you do." It comes out not sounding like a question, and while he thinks about how to respond, I quickly double back, "He did, and you do?"

"Yes, and yes."

"Can you tell me more? What sort of surgery?"

"You know, I'd rather not say, if you don't mind. Let's call it personal surgery. I have all the necessary medical documentation, if you wish."

Personal surgery? It smacks of student talk, and all I can do is show him my best annoyed face. "Ok, so what does all this personal surgery mean?"

"Of course, of course, but you know I am off to class, but when I return, for sure, when I return." And Ahmad, with purple bowtie, apologizes his way out the door.

6

Somebody's mother is at the door—*abaya, niqab*, black gloves—whispering, "May I come in?"

Because I slept funny last night—thinking that two pillows placed just right would make a difference, and they did until I woke up, my neck muscles refusing to work, ganging up about my shoulders—I cannot move my head from side to side. As I motion for her to sit, and she does, I stiffly lower myself into my chair.

There is a short quiet as she searches for that part of the chair that is best, and then, with a sigh, "Yes, well it is both simple and not so simple, *sah*. It has to do with Dana. Something is not right with my daughter, Dana. These days she returns from university in tears, upset. She rushes to her room. Dana does not eat. Something is all wrong I tell you. Terribly wrong. I see this every day. That is the simple part."

She fists a tissue and dabs at both eyes, even lifting her *niqab* to blow her nose.

"Yes, well, I can certainly see you are upset. How can I help?"

"It has to do with Professor Sara, I think. Yes, Professor Sara, the professor Dana believes is so very wonderful. You know the one?"

This is a surprise, and for the smallest moment I forget about the stiffness in my shoulders, my locked neck, asking, "You are sure about this? The professor part? Professor Sara, is it?"

"Oh yes, Dana said so. Her favorite teacher of all time, and now this; these daily tears and unhappiness that I cannot understand."

"Please, your daughter, what is her name?"

"Dana, Dana Mohammed."

"It is? Are you sure?"

She does not know how to answer this, and can only blink back at me.

"Yes, well, I mean, Dana is your daughter?"

"Yes, this is correct, Doctor. She has been my daughter for all these twenty years, twenty-one years next month."

Even though it is only the two of us and the door is shut, the hallway an early morning hush, I glance to see if we are alone, if others might have heard. Another lifting of the *niqab* and she blows long and hard. I say, "Please tell me more." I wince, my neck muscles biting.

"Yes, well, I will try but my daughter herself is not completely clear about this, and this is the not so simple part. Just the tears and locking the door to her room. But two days ago, the two of us sitting on her bed, she tightly holding on to her favorite pillow, she did say, 'She wants me to be somebody I am not. Doctor Sara wants me to be her, and although I want to be, I don't want to be. Cannot be—ever. Professors should know this. Of all people, professors should know this.' This I think is the key, Doctor."

I nod. "Yes, I see, I see," even though I don't. "I know your daughter, we all do. And yes, Dana is an excellent student, one of the very best I think."

It is then, as she nods in motherly appreciation, that the tissue rolls softly out of her hand and onto the floor. "Yes, good for my Dana, but after graduation she is all about getting married and having children, one boy, one girl, and moving into the grandmother's house, God bless her soul, *Allah yerhamha*. You see. It is all planned: husband, children, house around the corner, and now this . . ." holding up a tissue-less hand to show me a this, ". . . this Professor Sara thing; of course it is not really a thing, but what, what is the right word? Situation? Disturbance? Professor Sara wants my Dana to continue her studies, to go to the USA or maybe Canada, but to continue her studies somewhere, . . maybe anywhere."

"Yes, I know Dana, and her potential is massive." I surprise myself with the word massive, and even say it again, "Massive."

"But I tell you Dana is all about a husband and children; it has all been arranged, decided."

"Yes, yes, I do see."

"You do?" Her eyes extra-wide, and who knows, she might even be smiling.

"Yes, I think I understand. I will speak to Professor Sara about this."

"Fine. But one more small thing, professor: Dana does not

know I am here, and she must never know. Can you understand? If she finds out I spoke to you about this, about her, then . . .. I don't know what. But please, this is our secret, yes? You and me?"

"Yes."

She stands and holds out one black gloved hand. Her standing is faster than mine, and with tight, unwilling neck muscles, I struggle to rise and shake her hand. Her grip is surprisingly strong, not even a shake really, more like a tug. I gingerly shuffle to open the door but she is in a hurry and out the door and down the hallway before I know it. "Good-bye?"

Gently returning to my desk, resitting, I turn to look at her wadded tissue on the floor. I have no idea what to say to Sara. What? 'Please, Sara, stop insisting that our best and brightest students continue their studies. Please. What are you thinking? Stop.' Looking down at her white tissue on the floor, in front of my desk, my shoulders aching.

Later, before I leave, I head towards Simon's office. The Spanish adjuncts are playing their neverending Samba music; and although I don't hear their laughter, I know they are in there, behind a brightly-color *mardi gras* closed door. Again, Simon's door is sealed, and this time when I peek through his almost peek-proof window blind, I see he is not there. *Just as well.* I wanted his opinion, his advice about how to approach Sara, but, actually, what can he say that I haven't already thought about? The easy solution is to say nothing, to do nothing, because most assuredly Dana's angst will, like always, find a way to disappear and lose its sorrowful luster.

I near Sara's office, and although she is not there, I feel nothing like relief, just postponement of the inevitable.

ॐॐॐ

That night, at home, she asks, "How did it go today?"

She never asks me that, no longer, and all I can do is stop and stare. "What?"

"Today. How did it go?"

I think about this for a moment and then remember one of Bedour's new words, something she read in one of her 'fancy British novels.' "Swimmingly, today went swimmingly."

She frowns, saying, "Don't be silly."

I shrug and answer the answer of a high school student. "Ok. Nothing special."

She seems happy with that and even says, "Good."

I wait for more, as if she knows something I don't. For the rest of the evening, in mid-TV, I watch her closely for clues.

In the morning, of course, the first person I encounter is Sara, in the elevator, just the two of us.

"Morning."

"Yes."

Just as I decide to stop there, seeing my 'Morning' as more than enough of an early obligation, she turns full faced, asking, "And so?"

The elevator is especially lethargic, almost as if it does not have to go up if it doesn't want to. *You can't make me.*

"Yes," taking a deep breath, and so, "Well, you know I

had a visit from Dana's mother yesterday. Dana Mohammad's mother."

When she answers, "Yes, I know," I am not surprised. It is a small country, with everybody's cousin and uncle and aunt neatly woven into each other's universe, and I am no longer surprised as to whom knows what, when, or where.

"Yes, she is worried about her daughter, worried that. . . and here comes the delicate part . . . worried that Dana can't be you, as much as you would like her to be."

The elevator has arrived, a slow metallic yawn to empty us out.

"Yes, well, . ." all done looking at me, . . "Well, there you have it." And for the first time in a very long time, Sara smiles; and although it has nothing to do with me, I pretend that it does and smile back.

"Nice woman, Dana's mother. Minimal drama, just some of your basic motherly concern."

"Ok. Consider your work done: you have officially spoken to me about it. Mission accomplished."

I do not take kindly to this off-handedness, especially after her tantrum of two days ago. "You know, I didn't have to say a thing; I could have ignored everyone: Mom, Dana, you. Ignored the whole bunch of you."

"Yes, well, never mind," she says stifling a yawn, and she goes her way, me mine.

By the time I get to my office, I am angry; I feel sorry for the first person who will knock on my door.

❧❧❧

Saleh saunters into the classroom with hair at a cartoon slant, his face still unfolding from sleep. He steps to his seat in the back and plops down exhausted. I can only wonder what his nightly routine is: all-night video games, *shishah* gatherings until sunrise. Regardless, his morning depletion is something painful to watch as he struggles to keep his head up, and now leaning against the back wall, eyes closed, his mouth fish-like. The others pay no attention to Saleh, and he will periodically open his eyes to ask Mohammad what he missed, 'What's he saying?' And just as periodically, Mohammad will shake his head. I find Mohammad's head shaking more bothersome than Saleh's semi-conscious state. There is more talk about their research papers. Bedour is taking notes. Saleh stretches out at his desk like he is home, on the couch, and one last time he turns to Mohammad, asking, 'What have I missed?' Although they are at the back, against the wall, I watch Mohammad's mouth respond, 'Nothing.' In a very unprofessional way, I will remember this.

❧❧❧

When I see the three of them in the hallway, nonchalant and barroom-loud, I think about turning around and going back to my office, but at the last moment change my mind and even pick up speed to intercept them. They don't see me coming and when I arrive, leaning into their secret conversation, they are startled, and for some reason this pleases me. "Well, you know what they say," I announce.

Blinking back at me, until, "What?"

"Three faculty standing in the middle of the hallway like this, out in the open, talking, even laughing, pounding each other on the back, you know what they say."

Malcolm of Communication and Media repeats, "What?"

எ•எ•எ

In the hallway, the weekend looming, Marshall does three things: he sees me, grins a grin that, I have discovered, has almost nothing to do with happy, and hurries my way. "There is something I must tell you."

"Yes."

"Yes," and he launches into a lengthy confessional, admitting that he is on the verge of passing a student who deserves to fail, who rarely comes to class, who, if truth be told, has yet to do any assignment, who is more interested in video games than home-work, "and yet," pausing to give his blue dragon a good rub, "Yet, I'll probably end up giving him a token C. Imagine that."

I wait for him to finish before, "Ok, and why would you do that?"

A shrug, followed by, "Well when he does come to class he is by far and away the most interesting of the bunch, saying provocatively intelligent things, offering profound observations. When the mood strikes him, most articulate, this fellow. Again, he has not done any of the readings, scoffs at the assignments, but his insights are unique, original and thoughtful, and so yes, he is earning a C for potential. Yes, I like that, a C for potential."

Try as he must, Marshall can no longer do things to shock me, even handing out silly C grades.

"I see."

He is, as usual, hoping for more; even willing to endure a response on my part, but today, I am not in the mood for Marshall and his fleshy gang of dragons, and end the abrupt hallway meeting with an "Excuse me," and firmly, in a most chair-like-manner, stride away from him.

Today's newspaper is all about the legions of terrorists in Iraq, Syria and other assorted Middle Eastern countries. It is an old news that refuses to go away, and I no longer read the articles, a glance at the headlines is sufficient: beheadings in Syria, car bombs in Baghdad, executions by the dozens—men, women, children, cats and dogs. It really doesn't seem to matter as long as someone or something is killed. The news is in the taking of life, and I no longer find it surprising. Staying alive has become a violent pastime, and I am sometimes surprised that I have, so far, dodged the murder that swirls around me. To know that there are strangers out there dedicated to doing me harm, people I don't even know—will never know—is puzzling. To hold a grudge is one thing but to slice someone's head off because....

❧ ❧ ❧

Achilles turns to his mother Thetis and says, "No matter how much it hurts, I am going now to find the man who destroyed my beloved Patroclus. As for my own fate, I will accept it whenever it may be."

As I place the newspaper on the floor, out of the way, there is a knock at the door, and in steps Anwar.

All I know is Anwar's name, the rest is a shy *dishdasha* sitting quietly at the back of the classroom, next to the biggest and brightest window, talking to Farah who leggily sits in front of him, who seems to think everything he says is funny, or at the very least deserving a girlie giggle.

"Yes, Anwar, how can I help you?"

"Sorry to bother you, Professor."

"Quite okay."

"If this is a bad time, I can come another time."

"No it's okay. How can I help?"

"Yes, well, about the reading today."

"Yes."

"This Achilles fellow. There's something I'm missing because I can't understand why he's so angry…angry at everybody. What's he got against Hector?"

"You didn't read?"

"No, no, I did but it's a mystery. Achilles is too much, too angry, even for an ancient Greek, too much."

This is the most Anwar has spoken all semester, and I purposely wait, seeing if there might be more.

"Professor, . . ." rubbing his hands together as if he has a sudden urge for cleanliness…"Professor, what's he all about, this Achilles?"

"Well, for a start you may recall that Hector killed Patroclus, Achilles's friend. Remember that?"

"No, his friend you say?"

"Best friend?"

"And Hector killed him?"

"Yes, very dead."

Anwar smooths the sleeves of his *dishdasha,* both sleeves, followed by, "Then that explains everything? I see, Achilles should be mad, enraged. Yes, this is only right."

"It is?"

"Of course. Friends, family, if someone harms them, it is your duty to harm back. This is normal, *tabe'i.* Everybody knows this."

"I see."

"Patroclus you say?"

"His best friend."

He goes back to washing his hands in front of my desk. "Revenge is important, *muhim sah?* Without revenge, the fear of revenge, none of us would be respected, and if you lose your respect, then you have nothing."

"Is respect really so important?"

"It is the key to everything; without respect nothing else matters."

It is my turn to speak and I have much to say, maybe too much, so I say nothing.

"Achilles' best friend?"

"The very best."

"Very good, so Achilles was right all along."

"Is that a question?"

"*Lah, lah*, he was right, this Achilles, dead right."

Anwar's teeth are a strange milk-tooth small, and now that he has his answer, he shows them to me. "Yes, it all makes sense now. It all fits perfectly. Killing for revenge, for respect, the two go together, you see. One feeding off the other. Can I say that 'feeding off the other?'"

"Yes, I get your point. Good-bye, Anwar."

He backs out of my office, bowing Japanese-like as he goes.

Once the door clicks shut, I find myself glancing down at the newspaper on the floor, at the headlines.

ࠞࠞࠞ

The largest window in the house is in my study—what I call my study: one splintery picnic table with chair and computer, with small mounds of books, papers, magazines scattered, stacked, leaning. The trees are a dusty spring-bright while the neighbor's two yellow cats cruise the garden. There is a smear on the glass that is on the outside and unreachable. Farther down the street, I see someone sitting in his truck, windows rolled down, eating his breakfast, with morning newspaper. A tiny riot of leaves with sand whirls, . . . stops, . . . whirls, . . . stops, . . . whirls past his truck; and he stops eating, chewing, long enough to watch. From the upstairs window, letting my arms slowly unfold, craning my neck, now on tiptoes—hearing something like a popping in my ankles—I can see the traffic light on Abdullah Mubarak Street—a tiny rebound glaring back at me. A leaf, magenta and as big as my hand, bigger, flutters down. I watch it dip and twist and for a moment go magically up instead of down, but then, finally, getting it right, drifting down, disappearing. Holding up my hand, . . . and yes, the leaf is bigger. The man in the truck continues to sit, eat and read.

I am spending more time upstairs in the study, at the window, with the door locked. That, and I no longer feel guilty when they rattle the doorknob, asking when *Baba* will come out, wondering if they can come in, just for a while, until lunchtime, promising not to touch anything. Through locked door, I say, "No, later. Leave Daddy alone now." And while the twelve-year-old almost always gives up too easily—slouching down the stairs to tell Mommy that Daddy won't play, won't let them in, it isn't fair—the six-year-old hammers at the door, saying, "I want in right now. Right this minute." But even she—the one who can't understand why Cinderella doesn't have a last name—I won't let in. In the end, she, too, gives up, placing her little mouth against the doorknob, saying, "I don't friend you."

I never used to lock the door, but left it wide open, the girls rushing in to share a story, a complaint, to demand an answer: Why does Mickey wear gloves? Why is Pluto named after a planet? I never used to spend so much time at the window.

I hear somebody yelling outside and when I go to see who the yeller can be, there is just the early-morning dusty red brick buildings thataway, but no yeller in sight. Moving to where window meets wall and pressing my cheek against the glass, I can see the tip of the school down the street. A car has stopped mid-street to unload its children, the lavender-pajamaed maids scurrying to escort kids with backpacks into the school, while the driver—contently smiling into his cellphone—is happy to wait as a line of cars stacks up behind him, honking, but there's nothing to be done until the maid returns empty-handed, and even then, taking his time for a photo of the two of them—maid securely in the backseat. Since it won't be long—in fact here she comes now—the cars behind him can wait. More children are merrily trooping by, some of them squealing as they hurry because they are late, and the national anthem has already started, with what can only be a teacher leading the recital over the loudspeaker, little voices behind her doing their early morning national duty.

☙☙☙

Sometimes with nothing more than the whisky-light of early morning, I leave the house to make the slow walk to campus. As I walk the six blocks down and seven blocks over, the birds are just beginning their peepings; the same lanky jogger ambles by, and here comes the walker of dogs—a poodle and something re-sembling a hairy-brown scurry. On the corner three blocks down and three blocks over is a restaurant, and I sometimes go there to sit at the same table and eat the same breakfast—coffee with toast. Not even a breakfast really, just something for me to do while I sit and watch. The waitress who wears nylons on Tuesdays and a gold bracelet on Thursdays no longer asks me what I want. When she sees me through the window, she plunges through the big swinging kitchen doors and almost immediately re-plunges, carrying coffee and toast. She gets everything done in one visit: "Good morning. How are you? Here's your coffee. Enjoy." In a flutter of skirt—the rub-swish of nylons, if it's Tuesday—she shuffles to another table for more refills. It's right about then, when she bends just right, that I can see the lines of her panties; as she moves away, I can easily see the white of her bra, the way it clips at the back. All the while holding the coffee cup to my lips, sometimes sipping, sometimes not, I am almost certain I can see the brown of her nipples when she turns to laugh at somebody's joke— the way they've pushed through the stuff of bra. The hot coffee washes over my lips but I dare not sip, not yet. Of course nothing ever comes of it. It's nothing like that. Yet there's something in the watching and waiting and being patient, missing nothing, until finally I'll almost always spy a ripple of unclothed flesh, of elastic made visible. It's rewarding. That's the best I can do. It has to do with winning some kind of small, strange victory.

That night she screams at them to stop screaming, their voices booming up through the ceiling, my floor. My sweater has holes at the elbows and some mysterious stain at the neck. Standing at the window again, looking out into the bright night; some of the trees are stark, their branches witchy, as if they somehow missed the springtime memo, and if I look just right, I can see lights and windows of the apartment building two streets over. Our dog barks, and another answers. The screaming has not stopped. The floor quivers.

কিকিকি

What looks to be two brothers, friends, maybe cousins, follow her into my office. They are polite and stand half-in, half-out the door. When I invite all of them in to sit down, they smile. "*Shukran.*"

Sounding like a used-car salesman, I ask, "And what can I do for you today?"

The brother clears his throat and begins. He tells me his sister, motioning to the girl in chair three, has a problem with one of the English professors, and…. This is when I hold up a hand, like directing traffic, and say to him, to all three of them, "Can she speak for herself? I would appreciate it if I could hear from her."

"*Nam*, but as her older brother, as you know, it is my duty to get to the bottom of this."

I raise my eyebrows and look at him, wondering where he learned the 'get to the bottom of this'.

"Yes, I understand, but," motioning to his sister who has yet to have a name, "please let her tell the story. And she does.

The brother cannot help but interrupt every now and again to correct the story. Meanwhile, what can only be the other brother, the one wearing the whitest *dishdasha* I have ever seen, remains quiet, looking into his cellphone, now pushing buttons, only to glance up now and again to give the rest of us a sample of his attention. When she finally finishes and he reminds me that he only wants 'to get to the bottom of this,' I say, "I will look into it."

This is not a bad answer, and she, who still remains nameless, seems happy while the brother would like more immediate action. "Can I call someone else, maybe email? We will be back tomorrow."

I wait for his frenzy of brotherliness to run its course, before saying, "Please stop by this time next week. I will have better answers for you then. In one week."

Although one week is a long time for the three of them, I can tell by the way they fidget, converse, mumble, even consult their cellphones, that they understand they have no choice and amazingly like some sort of stage act, they all stand as one. "*Shukran.*" I shake hands with all three of them, the older brother twice.

ॐॐॐ

Nasreen doesn't come to class the Wednesday after her new short hair; it is the first time she has missed all term. Without her the class drones. I remind them about how examples and details are important to any writing, going to the board and showing them examples of examples, revisiting their very grammar school beginnings, the English-teacher talk they have heard for years. They look at me but even I can tell they are not hearing, seeing. And for the first time all semester, I am on their side.

Three days later Ahmad is back from his mysterious personal surgical procedure. He shyly knocks at my door before entering.

"Ahmad, welcome back. How are you feeling?"

When we shake hands, he hangs on. "Fine, fine but, . . ." fishing in his pocket with the non-shaking hand. ". . . but there is this," handing me a paper folded once, twice.

"What's this?"

Reluctantly letting go of my hand. "It's from the doctor, my doctor."

I unfold it once, twice, and read. In one long rambling sentence it says that, among other things, Ahmad needs rest, that his surgery was more serious than we thought but a success, thank God, but 'believe me when I say,' he needs rest, to recover, to get fully fit—two weeks rest would be best, more if possible. Respectfully. Like always, at the bottom of the page is a row of purple stamps, ending with something like an inky brush stroke for a doctor's signature.

"Two weeks?"

"That's what he said. Doctor's orders. I tried my best to change his mind, telling him there are classes to teach, papers to grade, meetings to attend, but, sad to say, he was insistent. 'Your health is more important than any of that,' he said. Twice he said that, maybe three times."

I hand the paper back to Ahmad and he refolds it into his pocket.

"Your doctor is right, about your health part. Very right."

For the first time since he walked in, Ahmad looks at me, smiling, his moustache a wispy stain. Thinking we are all done, that there's nothing left to say, or do, he leans to leave, but when we shake hands this time, I am the one who hangs on. His eyes widen, his smile waivers. Finally, "I will have someone cover your classes."

"Yes, yes, thank you, I owe you, surely I do," as he pulls his hand away.

All of this from a man who is notorious for denying medical excuses from students, because 'As we all know, five dinar can buy any medical excuse students want.' But more irritating is his last part, about owing me.

ও ও ও

Sara is heading to one of her conferences armed with the latest version of her Jane Eyre paper. She will miss two days, maybe three, and is seeking someone to take her classes, if they wouldn't mind. If not, per policy, she will have to make up the missed classes when she returns. She sent requests to her colleagues, and the last time I saw her she looked especially unhappy, prowling the halls for someone, anyone to confront. What this means is her request has been ignored. This, she will eventually come to tell me, is completely unacceptable. "Any other department on campus would show more camaraderie, more compassion, but no, not this one, not your department," and so on.

I ask, "Where's the conference?"

This catches her by surprise but not for long and in no time, she counters with, "You don't remember? You signed off on it three weeks ago."

Since this is nothing like a real question, I can afford silence.

Finally she sighs and runs fingers through her short almost-blonde hair. "Amsterdam. If you can't recall, it's Amsterdam."

"Aha, yes, of course. And all about Jane Eyre, is it, the conference?"

She waits to see if there might be more; she is ready and primed for more. But I can only offer her a smug Marshall-grin.

As she stalks away, she barks, "Your department. Your creation. Your Frankenstein."

She knows her Shelley, that Sara.

❧❧❧

The twelve-year-old, who is now full of 'no big deals…I have no ideas' and 'good for you', comes home hysterical. She cannot find her clarinet. She had it before she got in the car, had it in her hand, and now, now it's gone—disappeared, stolen, lost. How can that be?

In the beginning her sobbing is soft, half-hidden. I can hear her through the vents. But as she begins to think about it, the sobbing grows bigger. That, and *she* is there to remind her how much a clarinet costs, how much lessons cost. Does she have any idea? With mouth quivering, her face red and wet with tears, the twelve-year-old slumps to the floor. I don't have to go downstairs to know this is the scene; I've seen it before—six months ago with a kitten that, one May morning, decided to curl up and die behind the washing machine. The twelve-year-old squirming on the carpet, bumping into table legs, chairs. *My clarinet.* All the while Mother slants in the doorway, reminding her of the cost.

In the morning, before I begin my walk, I go to the garage, unlock the car, search and find the clarinet wedged in under the seat, among the springs and assorted gray plastic. I take it into the house and set it tower-like on the kitchen table. I will now walk the three blocks down and three blocks over with head down, crushing hundreds, maybe thousands, of leaves and twigs as I go. Once at the cafe, I am out of breath, the air refusing to go into my mouth fast enough. Two tables over, I listen to a man on his cellphone say he knows, "Don't have to tell me, I know." When he is all done, I can see he is not happy about knowing whatever he knows. For just the smallest moment I think about leaning over, even raising my hand, and asking him if everything is alright. But I don't…can't. He continues to frown down at his cellphone that he has placed on the tabletop, next to his plate of eggs and potatoes. He picks up a fork and then puts it back down.

The lovers in booth seven, under the Coca Cola sign, are giggling about their food (scrambled eggs with brown toast), their fingernails, her lipstick, his moustache … Everything is very funny. And when one of their forks clatters to the floor that too is funny. In fact, their giggling has become something organic, animal, like a tiny pet that has gotten away from them. If that were not enough, the wind is blowing extra hard and when people come in, the door refuses to close and tiny whirlwinds rush across the tables and countertop so the cook has to stop cooking to come out from behind the grill to give the door a good tug shut. They giggle. I've never been big on adults giggling. It is unhealthy. Course if you are in love that's something else and has nothing to do with health.

Meanwhile, the woman in booth 10 is frowning into her newspaper. Her scowl is serious and lawyer-like and when I look closer, yes, she has a briefcase at her side. Her newspaper is the same as mine but we are on different pages; she on the Business section, me the Sports. Glancing toward the kitchen, I see the cook, who has just returned from closing the door, is wearing a hairnet; sometimes I see him slip the hairnet off to scratch his head only to quickly snap it back on, as if he is being watched.

Wearing a hairnet is not a bad idea, especially if you are cooking other peoples' food, but then again if I were to swallow a strand of the cook's hair, I'd never know it, or probably even care. The lawyer woman in booth ten is angrily turning the pages of her newspaper until she stops at a large half-page photo. I can easily see from here that there has been yet another bank drawing contest, along with a long list of people who have won money. There is a photo of the winner standing next to what can only be the bank manager and together they cradle a large cardboard check for 5,000 dinar. The winner is looking straight into the camera and for some reason she does not look pleased, with a glare that says, 'Can we hurry this up, I've got to get to work.' On the other hand the bank manager is springtime smiling, as if giving away 5,000 dinar is a good idea. On that same page there is mention of marathons to be run, blood drives to be driven. Two new coffee shops have opened their doors and will be giving away free coffee to the first 100 customers.

It is then that a mother with young boy comes in, leaving the door windy wide open, and caring nothing for giggling lovers or frowning lawyers, she steps quickly to booth five—below the red no smoking sign—having not once stopped talking on her cellphone, laughing, "*Wallah, wallah,*" while her son, who not once pretends to know her, to sit next to her, decides to take a jaunt around the tabletops. Lowering the Sports section, I watch as he marches from one tabletop to the next, to the next, to the... When the mother finally stops talking long enough to look up and see him, yelling, "Mohammed, get down," he yells back, "No."

She shrugs a shrug that says, 'what's a mother to do', before going back to her cellphone, more laughter, more "*Wallah.*" By now, little Mohammed has reached table number twelve and is happily toe-ing the napkins holder, reaching down with pudgy fingers to see how much salt will fit across the tabletop. The cook looks up from his cooking, tugs at his hairnet and seeing boy on tabletop, says something in Tagalog to Eve. Eve hurries over to the boy to help him off the table, and he happily surrenders to her outstretched arms.

That is the waitress's name, Eve, her nametag says so. Eve always greets me with a "Welcome, it's a great day." She has been trained to say this, they all have, as if customers need reminding that such days do exist. But never mind, because she is simply doing her job, doing what she has been told; it is not her fault that her boss insists she recite such an awful greeting.

There is one fly in the café and it has found me, refusing to leave me alone. It crawls across my forehead, tiptoeing along my ear. It thinks nothing of stepping on my eyebrows. I shoo it away once, twice and even a third time. Secretly, I wish it would fly over to the lawyer woman; I'd like to see if she has a bigger, more ferocious frown.

By now the lovers have become strangely silent, the lawyer woman looking tired, as if all her frowning has, finally, caught up with her; in the meantime, little Mohammed with Mom are back together, she relentlessly chatting, he busily brushing salt from his fingertips.

If I hesitate any longer, I will be late, and like a kind of magic

Eve brings me my bill before I even ask for it. I pay and she reminds me one last time to have a great day, and I reply Okay. That's when I look up and see the café's light fixtures; there are twelve of them hanging from the ceiling like ancient salad bowls, a milky porcelain, one over each booth. After all this time and I had never noticed them before but now that I do and I stop to get a good look, I can see how they are a perfect fit.

When I give my coffee one last sip, something bumps up against my lips. Squinting to get a better looksee: a fly is floating perfectly dead, in what can only be a case of drowning by black coffee, without cream or sugar. Looking to see if others are watching, anything like a telltale smirk—and when I see nothing, I finger the fly out, flicking its body aside, and go back to sipping with a sigh—by now flies should know better.

❧❧❧

Suhail is quiet. I can't say he's shy because shy and quiet can be different things. That, and he never sits in the same seat twice. Just when I am used to seeing him on my right, next to the window, he shows up on my left. If illusiveness is his plan, it's a good one. Suhail doesn't ask questions, and I want to believe it's because he doesn't have to. When Suhail missed three classes in a row I asked others in the class if they knew where he had gone. "Where's Suahil? Who knows?" The response was an overwhelming, "Who?"

Suhail is regular. I have tried to assign him some sort of specialness but the only thing that comes is his silence, and that's nothing. He is medium height, not thin, nothing like fat, with dark hair and darker eyes. He has a habit of folding his hands on the desktop and leaving them there. Once I almost called on him during class to read just to hear his voice, but then, at the last moment, changed my mind. Sometimes when I am talking—students call it lecturing, I call it talking—I will hesitate and look at him, his neatly-folded, desktop hands, and when I do, he nods back.

After the three absences in a row, on a Thursday, Suhail comes to my office. He stands at my office door. When I look up, he asks, "May I come in?" and I motion him to a chair. He has shaved his head and his *dishdasha* looks strangely unwashed, stained, bruised at the elbows. He leans forward and folds his hands on my desk. We wait. Finally, taking a deep breath and running a hand over his blueblack shaven head, "I've done the *hajj,* you know."

His voice is just right for him: soft with a hint of correctness around the edges.

"Yes?" I say.

"Yes, my first time."

"Congratulations."

"Yes," hands back on the desk. "Yes, it was something."

"I can imagine."

"Well, . . ." when he stops to lift his head, to get a better look at me, I see a tiredness there that I hadn't noticed before. "Well, with all due respect, professor, unless you are Muslim, you probably cannot." The tiredness giving way to a blush.

We consider this for a moment, as cars honked, somebody yelling to wait, "Why can't you wait?" the call to prayer.

"You're probably right, Suhail. But surely you are not here to tell me this. Is there something else, something more? You missed classes and went on the *hajj*. Very commendable of you but now you are back. Is there something else?"

Taking his hands off the desktop and wiping them on his *dishdasha*, all the while glancing at me, now a peek at the window, the brown flat of the desk. "Yes, I think there is more—much more. This has opened my eyes, this *hajj*, professor, my eyes have been opened." And sure enough his eyes grow bigger, his eyebrows arching to make room.

I nod and he continues. "This..." holding out one hand to me, my desk, the book shelf and beyond. "This is not for me, I think. Before the *hajj* I didn't know, didn't suspect. How could I? Like all the others, I, too, walked dream-like, moving this way and that because I was supposed to, was told to, but now, . . now is not the time for me to care about things like thesis statements, or MLA citations, and what do you call it: dangling modifiers? This is not for me, maybe later. Much later."

He smiles as if sharing a joke and I smile back as if I know all about sharing jokes. And just like that he is done and stands.

"Wait, help me understand," I say. "This class is not for you? This is what the *hajji* has taught you?"

"Yes, well," a hand on the door as he gives me a disappointing look, an unspoken: is that the best you can do? "Yes and no, professor. It's larger than one class. One class is nothing."

"Larger? You're leaving school?"

"Yes, it is my decision. I must go north to help my brothers."

'Oh, you have family in Syria, Iraq?"

"*Lah, lah*," and for the first time I detect an unfriendly impatience in his voice. "No, not those kinds of brothers. The other, more important kind. My Muslim brothers need my help."

Only much later, after he had left, and there is yet another call to prayer, do I wonder what sort of help Suhail had in mind.

❧❧❧

The next night, during mid-shower, I look down and see a strand of white in the tangle of pubic hair. I quickly pluck it, thinking nothing of the tiny dot of pain that follows. I have strands of white hair on my head, on my chest, probably on my back. *But there?* I turn so the water will hit my back, leaving me alone with my one hair. I have never thought about white pubic hair—not once. Only when the twelve-year-old thumps at the door, saying she has to go, can't wait much longer, hurry, do I flick it from my fingers, watch it spin in the water, then cling to the side, now spin some more before disappearing into the silver-black of drain.

❧❧❧

Except for walks to the café and a sometimes taxi ride to the university, I stay home. But never mind because there's the local *bakalah* man around the corner who almost always goes out of his way to say, "Hello. How are you? Good to see you." But he doesn't mean any of it. In fact the words aren't even out of his mouth—half in and half out—before he's back to watching TV, sitting kingly on his stool behind the counter making sure the kids, who come in bunches of three or four, don't steal chocolate or handfuls of candy. I answer with "Hello…Fine…You too," and maybe buy some water, gum, a green bag of Regal potato chips. In the end, he does three things simultaneously: takes my money, says, yet again, "Good to see you," all while staring intently at the TV.

As I hurry home, I see some boy—no older than my twelve-year-old—drop a chewing gum wrapper on the ground. It isn't even a drop, more like a throw, and it's the throwing that makes me rush up to him, taking hold of his t-shirt, and in my best policeman voice, say, "Pick it up."

Almost home—another left turn—when one of the yellow jump-suited street cleaners with broom and garbage bag is standing in the shade, sees me and says, "Hi, boss." When I remind him, yet again, that I am not his boss, never have been, never will be, he smiles, as if he knows something I don't. Somebody has placed a handwritten note on the 24-hour pharmacy glass door that says it will open tomorrow, if not tomorrow then Tuesday for sure—*inshallah.*

When I get home my throat is throbbing; I hurry upstairs, lock the door and turn on the fan. Shaking my head, wondering what's going on, wondering why I can't get it right.

7

"*Nam? Nam?*"

"Yes?"

"Hello, yes, for your information, sir, Dr. Marshall Mullen of America has been arrested. For your information."

"Hello? Who is this?"

"*Nam,* this is Dr. Martin, of English classes at the university? The chairman, I think?"

"Yes, what is this about Marshall?"

"Arrested, sir. Very much arrested I am afraid. Thank you and good-bye."

I look at the telephone, then turn to the window, then back to the telephone that has not left my hand, and finally I take a brisk walk to Marshall's office that is locked. His hallway window is papered like something out of a World War II blackout. I scan the schedule on his door and he has no classes today. By now Ahmad has returned, in stoic recovery mode, and his door is open and two students are sitting there in silence. I offer Ahmad a token knock, saying, "Sorry to bother you Dr. Ahmad but have you seen Dr. Mullen today?"

The two students do not even bother to turn, to see who might be apologizing for interrupting, to see… Meanwhile, Ahmad, bow tied with neon pink shirt, is in full professorial form and in no hurry to answer. All four of us wait, until, finally, "Ahmad, have you seen Marshall today? This morning, anytime?"

This gives the two students a chance to toy with their cellphones, a thirty-second reprieve before Ahmad can start up where he left off.

"*Lah, lah*, no, I have not seen the man, not today, so sorry."

I offer a continue-with-what-you-were-doing wave, and move on.

Back to my office that now has a student standing obediently at the open door, and before I can wave her away, she asks, "Can I come in?"

"No, not now."

"Later?"

"Yes, later would be fine."

"When?"

"Tomorrow is best."

"But it's important, sir. Very important."

"Yes, I know, but tomorrow is my day for important talk."

"It is?"

I shut the door behind me.

I am looking at the telephone, waiting for it to do it again: to tell me more about Marshall, but it doesn't, it won't. I sit down and email others, asking if anyone has seen Dr. Mullen today or yesterday.

Only Ahmad replies.

I think about saying something to the dean, who is not here, a phone call to the president's office, but no, better to wait. Marshall has no classes today and tomorrow he has two, so yes, it is better to wait until he's officially MIA before scurrying to the authorities; on the other hand, . . . I picture Marshall with colorful dragons in a jail cell, and he is yelling, pounding the bars, demanding to speak to somebody, anybody. Me?

I call Marshall. No answer. Send him two, three emails, asking, "Everything ok?" No replies.

The next day I anxiously wait for his first class and when it is 10:00 I much too quickly go to the second floor, his class and when I open the door there he is: short-sleeved, unshaven, a rim of mud on his shoes. *Mud?* When he sees me, he glances back at his students, then back at me, asking, "Yes?"

"Everything alright here?" I say like some elementary school principal.

He answers "Of course" and his students seem to like this, twittering as if they know something I don't.

Later, I will catch him at the mailboxes. Now that he is without an audience, I ask again, "Everything alright?"

This time he answers weakly, less professorial, "You sound like somebody's third grade principal."

"I know."

Now that I have him in front of me, I can see there are scratches on his cheek, behind his ear, a red swelling around his eyebrows. "Long weekend?"

Marshall locks his mailbox, which surprises me; I didn't take him to be the mailbox- locking sort. He rubs his arms, his dragons, and says in a most un-Marshall way, "You have no idea, Mr. Chairman. No idea."

"Anything you want to talk about?"

"No, sir, nothing I want to talk about." But before he walks off, it's almost as if he needs to remind himself that, . . . "Oh, by the way, you can't be caught out in the open like this, in full frontal view. Be careful."

He is almost to the elevators when he glances back at me, and it is in that glance—a half-look that the old Marshall would never do—that I understand just how long his weekend was.

ھ ھ ھ

Nasreen hasn't stopped sitting in the back, between Mohammad and Yousef. She spends much of the class looking at her hands, her new jewelry. Her black hair is slowly growing back. Another Wednesday, and I let them leave early, and they are happy, even thankful. One of them comes up and says, "Thank you." I am not sure how to take this, and simply say, "You're welcome." Only Bedour looks worried. Before Nasreen has a chance to leave, I arrange myself near her, under the clock, and as the others shuffle out, I ask how she is. She answers in a whisper, "Fine." It is the sort of one-word answer that is meant to appease, to halt all further questions. I notice that she is without her necklace, the red string, the piece of jade.

After Nasreen, my jungle dreams slowly give up. I have one

last sweaty visit in April, near Easter. I remember the creepers taking on a life of their own, magically snaking down and around to grab my arms, squeeze my legs; slithering noose-like around my neck. I wake sputtering, coughing. She mutters what sounds like a question. When I peer out the window, there is the blush of sunrise.

As Spring Break nears, Peter and Sara both wave as I hurry by their offices, even murmuring something that sounds suspiciously like a Hello. As department chair, I am duty-bound to hi them back and even think about backing up to, perhaps, say, "Good morning," but no, I am in a hurry. When I get to my office and stare into my computer, I cannot recall what the rush was—is—but never mind because I call Reedah to ask her. "Reedah, what do I have to do today?"

"Good morning, Dr. Martin."

"Yes, yes, morning. Remind me, what am I doing today? Something important I bet. Tell me."

Reedah is good at big silences, but this time I can't wait for this one to run its course and I give her a breathy John sigh, which works. "There's the usual, nothing urgent."

"Are you sure?"

"Dr. Martin, there is nothing, I tell you, and, . . . oh so sorry, Registrar is on the other line. I'll call you back."

Reedah is good at ending her telephone talk this way: 'Let me call you back.' Of course she never does.

The spring break-nearing mood can be felt in students, too. Students who I don't know—will never know, and don't even recognize as students but must be because there they are walking around the campus—say, Hello and Good morning, Doctor.

I respond, "Yes, how are you?" One student actually stops to shake my hand and tell me, since I asked, how he is. After one "I see" and two "Is that right" I tell him I must go, am late for a meeting, and he apologies for keeping me, for answering my question, and we go our separate ways after he offers me his strongest heart-felt handshake, ending with a McDonald's "Have a nice day."

৵৵৵

Not only is the 24-hour pharmacy still closed, but the newspaper—page two, column one—tells me that a sea captain of some 33 years fell overboard and drowned. But there's more: birds are not paying attention—thinking of other things—and flying into trees, colliding with buildings and various monuments. Just the other day two pigeons, one right behind the other, flew straight into the water tower—a star burst of red and feathers.

What happened to the good old days, when sea captains knew better than to drown, and birds—heads up—knew what was what. Something happened—between there and now—something happened and I'm not sure what to call it, the name for it, except it happened— and if I could vote it away I would, or if I knew what government office to send my letter of complaint to I would. Until then, the 24-hour Pharmacy will remain closed, 'Man overboard', drivers will continue to take up two parking spaces instead of one, as plastic bags along with wind-driven fast-food wrappers pile up next to empty garbage cans, and so on.

Later, I ask the lovers to stay after and see me, and when they do I begin. "Why do you want to wear jeans with gaping holes at the knees? Does it have something to do with migrant workers? No? With the homeless? No? Then perhaps it's symbolic, a metaphor of sorts?" And all they can do is stand soldier-still, open-mouthed, shaking their heads. "What, then, is the advantage of looking war-torn and dispossessed, like some Eastern European refugee? You've been to war? No? Then you've seen war—what bullets and bombs can do? Have you ever seen the beast of battle outside the fluff of newspapers and films and. . . . ? No, of course you haven't. Have you heard the screams, seen what napalm can do to flesh and bone? Seen what it does to babies? Do you even know what napalm is? No, again. You just know about jeans with holes in the knees and baseball caps worn backwards and earphones screwed into your ears, and. . ." Speaking in a soft even voice, lecture-like, looking them straight in the face so they won't forget. All the while, he, a pimply boy, and she, a not so pimply girl, have not stopped being wide-eyed, moving only to nod at the right time. Finally, as another class begins to filter in, she clears her throat and says, "Yes, we see. Will that be all, Professor?"

Not much time later, once back in my office, with door firmly locked, head in hands, thinking, *No, no, that wasn't it either. Not even close.* I reach to turn off the lights so it will look like the office is empty.

Taking my time walking home, taking the backstreets, hands

in pockets, not thinking of anything special except walking, watching the dirt in front of me change from brown to gray and back to brown, when suddenly a gray cat jumps out from one of the garbage dumpsters. In one furry fearful motion it sees me, hisses and scats. All of this brings me to a breath-catching halt as I stumble. The gray cat, ears back, now safely under a car, glares back at me, as if whatever happened was my fault.

At the corner I take a right to a main street, my heart racing. And when I do a black truck rolls up onto the curb, onto the sidewalk, startling three walkers, who slow, stop, mumble and frown, then veer left. The driver, sunglasses, firmly clutching a cellphone, throws open the truck door and steps out, declaring to anyone who will listen, "I'm in a hurry. I won't be long. I'm in a hurry." On second thought it is not clear if he is speaking into his cellphone because now, he laughs at what can only be someone's joke. "I'm in a hurry, behind schedule, you know." Meanwhile, the walkers, like water flowing around a boulder, must bend around him and his black truck.

When I get home there is a small electric fan at the end of the picnic table and I switch it on. I wait for its humming to warm to words. Etched into one of my biggest knuckles is something like a liver spot—brown, stain-like; I don't remember it being so large. The fan is now humming, pushing cool air first this way, then that; blowing cool air across my face and then coming back to do it again and again, it speaks: *Good to see you. Good to see you. Good to see you. Good to . . .*

The next morning Ros announces that she will be out of the

office for three days. This, we know, is good because for three days there will be no meetings, no urgent emails. When the dean is away there are no emergencies and we will not have to sing "Row, Row, Row Your Boat."

At exactly 9:04, grade-appeal Maryam is at my door.

"Good morning, Professor."

"Yes?"

"Can I talk?"

"Will it be a long talk?" Although it is far too early for any type of student unhappiness, I motion her in anyway. *Is it possible she has no unhappiness to share with me?*

"Professor, I am really upset."

"The grade appeal decision, is it?"

"Yes, of course there's that, as well as so many other things, but we can just start with the grade appeal." For the first time I notice that Maryam has a button-nose and a cluster of freckles on her chin. When she talks, her entire face hurries to the center. "Their decision was wrong, you know. So really wrong."

"Because they denied your appeal?"

"Yes, but it's not just that. So, what else is to be done? Is there a next step?"

I place both hands flat on the desktop and say, "I think you are done."

But she cares nothing for the flatness of my hands, asking, "An appeal to the appeal?

Professor, he called me a girl, twice. Really. In front of the class, my friends, he called me a girl."

"Maryam, I thought we were talking grade appeal. You are talking about something else, something different."

When she smiles, the gang of freckles neatly line up under her lip. "I know, but like I said, there are just so many other things, don't you think? Professor, he called me a girl—twice."

I look to the cluttered corner of my office, to the vanilla-colored portable heater squatting there. All those many Augusts ago when I first arrived, the oven-like heat of when I stepped out of the airport was brutal, all the while thinking this can't be right, even for the desert, something, somewhere must be broken. Days later, introduced to my fifth-floor office and seeing the heater in the far corner, I finally had to ask in questioning disbelief, "Is that a heater?" The answer being, "Yes, of course." Still in disbelief, saying, "You're kidding, a heater?" And the HR fellow, who was only doing his job and anxious to return to his air-conditioned office, job all done, "Yes this is your office," touching the heater with the tip of his shoe, ending with, "Believe me, in January and February this will come in handy." He was right; in fact....

"I mean, really, even my father doesn't call me girl. My own father."

"Maryam, there are far worse things to be called, with girl being very low on the insult list."

"Maybe, Professor, maybe. But on that day, in that class, with everybody silently watching and listening, it was number one on my list. Girl, Number one."

Later that afternoon, the neighborhood security sirens wail to see if they work and they do, and people hurry to the windows to see what is what, but it is only a test: page two of the newspaper in bold print, announcing: "Testing Security Sirens Today."

The siren testing all done, as I leave the bathroom, risking the long hallway before the right turn to my office, I see the three of them, John, Peter and Marshall, huddled in mid-hallway. This, I believe, is a first; this threesome gathering at something that is not an official meeting. I stop, see if they see, and they do not, and quickly return to the bathroom, standing in front of the mirror to lean closer, since I am here, to see what I might have missed shaving, wondering how, overnight, that white hair got there, yanking nose hairs out by the roots, and if I ever so slightly lift my chin to the left that ridge of wrinkles neatly disappears, . . . Finally, I am ready to try again, and this time, to my surprise there are four of them: John, Peter, Marshall and Ahmad. I move towards my office, as if this is normal; I even speed up to meet them. As I arrive, they stop talking to say, Hi, Hello, Hey, Mr. Chairman. As chair I consider parking myself neatly into their mid-hall gathering, but with arms across chests, along with much shoe shuffling, the signal is clear: 'That's close enough,' and the best I can do is hold up a hand, 'Gentlemen,' picking up speed to continue on. I feel them watching me as I take the corner.

I saw the flash from the window, followed by a boom and then almost immediately a black smoke. I waited for more, for the mistake to be corrected. The black smoke mushrooming straight up. All of this from the hotel across the street. The telephone rings and I hurry to answer, "Yes?"

"Did you see that?"

"Yes? You mean the explosion? What was that?"

"Did you see that?"

"Who is this?"

"See that?"

"Who is this?"

By now cars are stopping, people running. There are loud voices in the hallway. I await our Nepalese security guards to come running down the hallway, rapping on doors, insisting we leave, now, 'What waiting for?' But nothing.

This is the second explosion in as many months. The first didn't count: somebody's car at the intersection catching fire and it, along with its gas tank, going up in a grand yellow puff of smoke and glitter. All the while the driver, hair startled, shoeless, frantically pacing the sidewalk, screaming into his cellphone. But this explosion is different, and within minutes the police, guns drawn, are in the street, stopping traffic, telling pedestrians to stand over there, hands up. 'What's in the bag?'

Our Nepalese security locks the gates, their cellphones at the ready. The telephone rings again but when I answer nobody is there. There are fire trucks and more police with guns, and now two hovering helicopters. All the while, the smoke is churning bigger, taller, blacker.

The next day the newspapers will say it was nothing more than a kitchen explosion, gas cylinders too close to a hot stove, killing one cook and various kitchen help in the hotel. *Nothing to worry about.*

Meanwhile, up north, or almost north, some 500 or 600

kilometers thataway, therc is continual warfare and misery on a grand scale: daily car bombings, kidnappings, random shooting because people belong to the wrong clan, sect, tribe, religion. The mass of death and dying has not filtered down this far, not yet; of course we can't help but wonder if one morning we will wake to tanks in the streets, plumes of black smoke slanting across the sky, oil installations under siege. The bake of the desert sun keeps all of us indoors but in the evening, crowded coffee shops, *shishah* bars, restaurants have become targets. Violence is a language we understand, and the very hint of it will send us scurrying to the airport, to escape to anywhere but here. *The heroics of Hector—no thank you.*

❧❧❧

On the eve of Spring Break, there is, like always, a rush to get to the airport. Faculty call in sick while students are already halfway to London, or Dubai. Out of a curiosity that is more than dull chair duty, I visit classrooms, showing my face at door windows, to see who is there, and who isn't. Nothing like noting times and names, it is not that kind of curiosity, and yet, admittedly, it doesn't hurt to remember.

John has sent me an official memo announcing his illness (sore throat and general stomach unfriendliness) and cancellation of classes for the day. Shortly after his memo I receive fewer official notices from Ahmad and Marshall making similar announcements (one, reminding me that he is still under doctor's orders; the other, just because). Either way, they have decided to cancel classes. As the quiet afternoon wears on, a tall, cowboylike, James Deanish student appears at my door.

"Yes, can I help you?"

"Yes, you can. Where is my professor? He is not in class. There is some kind of note on the door saying class is cancelled, but why?"

I say, "Yes, he is not feeling well."

I don't know the instructor, the class, but my answer covers all, on this the afternoon before the Spring Break.

"Well, excuse me, but this is the third time he has cancelled class and excuse me but I am paying money for him to be in class. He is always ranting about our attendance when, excuse me and with all due respect, I am beginning to question his."

I like his logic and wait for him to go on but he seems happy to stop, having made his point.

I say, "Good point, but you know even professors have bad days, traffic accidents, grandmothers dying, illnesses." Shrugging to show him what a professor's bad day looks like.

"Yes of course, but don't you have something like makeup classes for those classes that are missed? I think something like that is only right, don't you?"

Because I like this tough cowboy talk, I look closer, longer at him. Tall, thin, jogging shoes, a T-shirt that reads T-SHIRT. He takes both hands to push back his hair.

"You are not wrong, and I was under the impression that all faculty who do miss classes, whatever the reason, do hold some sort of makeup classes, but you are telling me no, not so?"

"Correct."

Any other time this 'correct' answer would be an irritation but with this fellow, this lanky James Dean, I find it charming.

"What is your name and who is your professor?"

"My name is Jasson, with two s's and Dr. John is my professor."

"I promise you I will look into this, Jasson with two s's. Promise. Please come see me after the break."

"Excuse me, but I will." And we shake hands.

After that I shut my door, lock it, and double check the window blind to make certain there are no open seams for others to look in.

Later, I meet Peter coming out of the Diner and ask, "How goes the project, the book contract? Any news?"

"Ready for this?"

"You mean the sirens, bells and whistles of yesterday? Never get used to things like that, never. They say it was an accident, something about kitchen mayhem, something about. . ."

"No, no," he interrupts. "Not that," motioning nowhere in particular.

"Oh, I thought, . . . Then what?"

Peter sighs a sigh that means I should have guessed by now. "They tell me that sort of editorial issue has brought everything to a halt. A screeching halt, and they are taking a second look at the manuscript. I believe the word they used is 'reassessing.' Yes, I am sure that's the word, 'reassessing.'"

"You're kidding?"

"'Fraid not. Got the email this morning."

"Did they say why? Anything?"

Scratching his chin with both hands, as if it's a big itch that no one hand can handle, he says, "Well, there's more, something about 'rehashing of an old well-worn thesis'. I have it here somewhere if you're interested," and he begins to forage through his pockets.

"Not necessary. But that's amazing. Just amazing. I'm sure something can be worked out. Can you make the necessary adjustments? Squash this reassessment talk?" Putting on my best wounded-face look, even holding fingertips to my lips, "What's to be done?"

Back to scratching his chin that is now red. "Don't know. 'A dungeon horrible, on all sides round.'" His scratching all done, he looks me straight in the eye, whispering, "And quite frankly I no longer care. Really do not."

This, I know, is a lie. But I nod like it isn't.

Thinking all is done, he takes a step, readying himself to move on, leaning toward the elevators.

I genuinely feel sorry for Peter. He's a terrible classroom teacher, but certainly has to be one of the top Milton people there is, *sans* any Milton book. I fear this editorial issue will throw him into a funk that will reverberate throughout the department. To think more about Peter's plight, I trek to the fifth floor, lock my door and swivel to stare out the window, into the Gulf. The telephone rings once, which usually means somebody misdialed. Minutes later it rings again—once.

෴෴෴

"Like always, please put away your machines; for the next 45 minutes you will be out of touch with the rest of the world." And like always there is a general shuffling of electrical gadgetry as they rearrange themselves.

At two seats over, three chairs back, Haya, too, goes through the motions of putting her cellphone away. Yet, once we begin— as I invite them to wonder why the good doctor thinks a red wheelbarrow with white chickens is so important, or why Mr. Frost should care about which road anybody takes—Haya is busy glancing down into her open purse where she has carefully placed the cellphone just right. And so, right in the middle of considering how people on the metro can look anything like petals on a branch, I stop and stare at Haya—a teacherly glare that says I know what you are doing but notice how I haven't said anything yet—thinking that will be enough, and sure enough, she will look up, read my eyes and for another three maybe four minutes, aim straight ahead, pondering what Chopin's Mrs. Mallard's weak heart is all about or what's this talk of a lottery prize being death, until, eventually, the urge overwhelms her and giving me a 'what's a girl to do' blink, she looks down long and hard into her gaping purse.

Eventually, some twenty minutes into the class—and I have just declared Hemingway an okay writer, but "he wrote better when I was younger"—Haya raises her hand and says she is not feeling well. When I ask what's wrong, she gingerly places a hand over her stomach, and I say I see but she says it again, "Not feeling well at all, sir."

"Yes, that will never do."

By now, with cellphone having moved from purse to hand, where even I can see a green light blinking, she will ask, "May I go? Go to get better?"

Not too long ago, someone once told me more about Haya, insisting that something was not entirely right with her, that, 'sad to say,' she was more than attached to her cellphone, something bigger, more sinister; that's the word that was used—'sinister.' But that someone—who now that I think about it was most certainly a she—went on to say that: *When Haya showers, she has a special place for her cellphone, you know, a neatly taped plastic pocket just the other side of the shower door, so, if necessary, all it takes is a quick wipe of misty shower glass and she can see who's texting, calling, what important red and green lights are blinking. But then, one day last November, when she least expected it, Haya's cellphone disappeared, and for the longest time she spent the day useless, hopeless; the unfairness of it all was unimaginable; she was lost in what can only be described as a mild panic. But never mind, because in the end, after hours of frantic searching and re-searching, Haya finally located it, caught between invisible mini pockets in her purse. The homecoming was tearful and to celebrate, that night, the two of them went to dinner, she places it on the table, atop a very white napkin where she could watch it closely.*

Looking back on it, I should have asked, "How can you possibly know all of this?" But I didn't and just nodded.

But by now, like always, I have lost interest in Haya and look down at my notes. In her classroom world my looking down is as good as a yes, and so she unfolds herself from the desk and walks out. I watch her go and try as I may I want to be angry, but nothing comes of it. Turning to the class, "Where was I?"

And Khalid, being Khalid, reminds me, "Hemingway, sir, an ok writer, sir, but better when you were younger, sir."

Later, I will see Haya at the Diner with friends, laughing and taking selfies, apparently her stomach problem solved, and she is missing our discussion as to why Willy Loman never a chance.

❧❧❧

The dean has returned from wherever she went and before the morning is finished, she calls.

"Hi, welcome back," I chirp.

"Thanks so much. Say, I need to speak with you as soon as possible."

I pick up the yellow pencil that I have never used, will never use, its eraser a healthy meaty pink. "Is it urgent?" I ask, already knowing the answer.

"Yes," she answers, and I can hear her licking her lips. "Yes, I believe it is."

"Once I finish with this student I will come over. Give me five minutes."

"Fine. Take your time."

She doesn't really mean this take-your-time part, but it is what we say. Finally, after ten minutes, I move in her direction.

"Listen, there is a complaint."

"There is?"

"Yes, it's not serious, but a complaint nonetheless."

"I see."

A short deanish silence ensues but is quickly filled with a telephone ringing, hallway laughter, a low-flying fighter jet rattles the windows.

"It's against you. The complaint, against you."

I feint a nod of non-surprise.

"Martin, would you like something? Coffee? How about a cup of coffee?"

"Some black coffee would be fine."

She dials the tea-boy who suspiciously appears at the door almost immediately: a tea for her, coffee for me, thank you so very much.

"What's the complaint? Peter, is it? More Marshall unhappiness, I suspect."

"Oh no, nothing like that. This is a student."

I watch for a smirk, the slightest hint of a joke, but. . .

"Really?" Rewinding the last couple of days, thinking of what it could be, who it could be, what I said, or didn't. But nothing smacks of complaint.

"Yes, apparently you were rude to a student. That's what he said "rude" or maybe "very rude", but you get the idea. Anyway, he insisted that I speak with you—something like a reprimand, I suppose. He said he feels like a formal complaint. Again, his words, 'I feel like a formal complaint. Is there a form to fill out?'"

The low-flying jet has returned, an airy growl, and windows flutter and rattle. She rolls her eyes skyward, "What's this about?"

"What?"

"With the jets." Are we under attack? Barbarians at the gate? Some national celebration we forgot about. Military exercises? What?"

"No idea. More middle eastern mischief, I suspect."

"But let's back up: his words are 'rude' to 'very rude'. What's that about?" she wonders.

"No idea. Guess we have different definitions of rudeness. But surely there must be more."

"Yes, well, ok, something about he missed classes because of an illness and you did not accept his medical excuses. Ring a bell?"

"Ah yes, that fellow. The one who believes a semester should be compressed into six weeks. He complained? Truly amazing."

She leans back in her dean chair, high heels crossed. "His tale is different from yours?"

I give her an are-you-serious look. "Ros, are we dealing with a *wasta* issue here? This student knows someone, who knows someone. . . ?" I want the low-flying jet to return, to rattle the windows, to send people scurrying under their desks. She fingers the stack of papers on her desktop.

"Ok, here's the story: for the first six weeks of the term, student comes to class off and on, so far so good, and then—and this is the important part—and then student disappears not bothering to resurface until the very last class of the semester. No emails, no telephone calls, no contact—nothing. And now, after missing...

wait for it…after missing some ten weeks of class, he appears seeking special consideration because of what, illness? I asked him if he were in the hospital, in a coma, maybe unconscious, with multi-colored tubes running down his throat, in his ears, up his nose? No he was not, but never mind because he is here now, the last day of classes and please do magic. He doesn't say the magic part but that's what he wants. When I say no, he, like always, wants to debate, to negotiate, to bargain, to whatever, but I have no time or patience for such silliness and I tell him, 'We are done. Good-bye.' He, one last time, attempts to launch into some sort of 'do me a favor' speech and I hold up a hand, saying once again but with much more gusto, 'We are done. Good-bye.' So, if that is rudeness, then 'yes, your honor', guilty as charged."

"I see, well," stretching her lips to stifle a yawn, looking down at her hands, turning them this way and that. "Well, still, you may hear more about this. Never know."

"Fine, let the rudeness wars begin." I unseat myself and move toward the door, asking, "Is that it?"

She goes back to the stack of yellow and white papers on her desktop. "Have a nice day."

The teaboy is at the door with coffee and tea; he looks confused, as if he has done something wrong and now that I am leaving, without coffee, how can he make things right. When I grab the black coffee she owes me from his tray, the jet fighter returns, extra loud, angrily low; the floor quivers, windows shiver, and something, somewhere breaks. With coffee firmly in hand, I find all of this wonderfully pleasing.

ॐॐॐ

Thomas Chapel is at the door, and when I motion for him to sit, he will not, but instead sticks his hands deep into his pockets, announcing, "Something not right, you know. Students, campus mood, faculty doesn't care...something gone all wrong."

I can't imagine how when he looks in the mirror, he cannot see that one of his nostrils is all wrong, the way it leans to the left as if it doesn't care. Now that he is here, I have forgotten all about his eyebrows: a grand bushiness, tipping into his eyes. Thomas pulls at his earlobe, a pink slab that serves no meaningful purpose. He lifts a hand out of his pocket to finger a book on my desk, turning pages.

When I first met Thomas, I made the mistake of calling him Tom.

'Do I look like a Tom to you? I mean, really? A Tom? Isn't that the name of a cat, a cartoon cat? Tom and Jerry, is it? Thomas is my name. My name is Thomas, thank you very much.' When I apologized, he answered with a 'quite right.'

Thomas takes a step back, outlining himself neatly in the doorway. Hands back in pockets. "It's not the same, that's all. Things aren't what they used to be: students, faculty, this place. All new and gone sour, I think."

This is the most Thomas has spoken to me in semesters, and for the first time, after all these years I am happily startled: he has a hint of a lisp?

"Well,. . ." scratching an earlobe, "well, there you have it." As he walks away, I fight the urge to call him back.

Later that afternoon I return to my office to find a fist-size pile of sand on my desk. It is a very compact, well-organized pile, and for reasons I will never be able to explain, I find it fitting.

8

Another Gulf country king has died, this one at the age of 91. It was not a surprise and the TV stations play mournful music all day and the next and part of the next. Once the three days of mourning is officially declared, there is, once again, a rush to get to the airport, to get to Dubai or Abu Dhabi, a quick shopping spree in Istanbul. As a show of respect and general sorrow, all entertainment is postponed, the cinemas close at sunset, restaurants, coffee shops and *shishah* bars are requested to refrain from playing music. Soccer matches are rescheduled. The newspapers say the new king is the dead one's half-brother. There are photos of both of them—front page. The newspapers run special editions, giving ten pages of photos and history of the dead king. When asked if the new king will make any changes—will oil continue to flow, will international affairs remain stable, can terrorism be defeated—the answer is three yeses', with an *inshallah* thrown in for good measure. Because the new king is 82 years old, in another four or five years there is an unspoken understanding that three days of mourning will be repeated. However, in the meantime, the airports are crowded, the roads full as families rush to the beaches, to their chalets.

When I get home, Jaffar and Jacob have assumed their positions on the stools, in the shade, smoking and drinking tea.

"Hello."

"*As-salam aleekum.*"

Between their stools is the empty soup can that is their ashtray. The dog, hearing my voice, barks. The three of us make a neat triangle; they sit, sandals off, me holding an empty briefcase. When the dog comes to the gate, whining to be let out, a lizard scampers across the pebbles and up a nearby palm, stopping at mid-trunk to clockwork its face our direction. Jacob smiles. The dog is trying desperately to wedge its nose under the gate, blowing dust and sand and now digging to be let out. Jaffar gives me a thumbs up, announcing, "Your car ok. Cleaned inside and outside. No problem, *sah*. No problem today."

"Yes, that is good, thanks so much for that." A soft doggy moan with nose wedged under the gate.

I find myself staring at Jaffar's feet that he has youthfully pulled up onto the stool; they are a walnut brown and almost shovel flat; where toenails should be is something else, something horny, a buttery yellow slanting to the right. I can see where once upon a time Jaffar had hair, a ghostly hairline etched into his scalp. When he is not smoking and laughing, he is running a hand over that once-hair.

Once I open the gate, the dog immediately loses interest and trots off into the shady part of the garden. Although it is nothing like nighttime, not yet, Jacob leans back and says, "Good night, Dr. Martin." Jaffar thinks this is funny: lighting a cigarette with one hand, rubbing his head with the other, laughing. I look for the dog but it is nowhere to be seen.

శ్రీశ్రీశ్రీ

From my fifth-floor office window the city haze has once again leaked into the Gulf. Someone is jet-skiing, as two very white boats move nonchalantly from left to right. A ghostly oil tanker simmers on the horizon. Behind me is the hum of hallway talk, while somebody's telephone rings and rings. This is about the time the morning hospital shift is all done and walks this way to the bus stop, two lines: one Indian, one Filipino. But today I don't see them and I wonder if I am early or they are late. In the end my thoughts turn to Jane Eyre and Sara.

శ్రీశ్రీశ్రీ

Christopher Owen of history department fame has announced his retirement. Christopher has always been a favorite with students because he cares nothing for attendance, has no problem with them using cellphones and other handy machines during class and is notorious for letting the girls have their way with him. On the other hand, when it comes to committee work, he is the one who knows all there is to know about Roberts' Rules of Order, and if meetings do not adhere to this standard, he has been known to bring any and all discussion to a screeching halt until it is done properly. Christopher is a cretin of the first order and he knows it but at this stage of his career, the end, he cares little what other people may think, except, the pretty girls in his classes.

I send him an email congratulating him on his retirement. He responds, saying he will slip away to his villa in Cyprus, in the hills above Paphos. I congratulate him again. Christopher is stubby-short and bald and holds his clothes together with red suspenders that, fittingly, only serve to make his bald head appear balloonish. With news of his pending retirement, there is, I sense, a wave of mild, controlled celebration among those of us who have been saddled with him in committees over the years. And so Dr. Owen and his groundbreaking work on the History of the Belgium Congo, listing, among other things, King Leopold's many crimes against humanity, not to mention the African rivers and forests, will be leaving us at the end of the semester.

Bedour wants to know if she can come in and I say she can. She then wants to know if she can have a seat and I say she can. Bedour has a serious face; I have never seen her smile, at best a hint of a grin. "I am worried, Professor."

"Yes, well, there can be a lot of things to worry about, don't you think? What particular worry did you have in mind?"

"Please don't make fun of me. I hate that."

Folding my hands on my desk, I lean closer, saying, "Sorry."

"I am worried that I am not learning anything in your class. Everything we talk about, everything you have taught us is not new to me; I have heard, learned all of this before, in high school, maybe even grammar school. Please give me something new?"

With anyone else I might feel offended, but with her, she might be right; still, "It's too early to tell, Bedour."

"Sorry?"

"Whether you are learning anything, it is too early to tell. Sometimes it doesn't arrive in a rush, overnight; sometimes it takes days, weeks, even years. It is too early to tell. Don't be so impatient."

I think this is a good answer but she is not convinced. "Maybe." Rubbing her eyes with the back of her hands, making her look older, no longer the teenage stuff of college students.

"Bedour, are you ok?"

"How do you mean?"

"I don't know, but ok?"

"Yes, but I simply want bigger and better learning; I don't want to waste my time, you see."

And with Bedour I do see.

"Anyway, I think I am done; I just wanted to, . . .wanted to . . tell you. Are you mad? Please don't be mad."

"I am not mad. With someone else, yes. With you, no."

For the very first time Bedour leaks a smile.

Bigger and better learning?

❧❧❧

Across the street live people who had no idea that one day a university would be built directly across from their front porches, that their balconies would overlook a row of classroom windows, that if they timed it just right, they could pull back their bedroom curtains and watch the occasional professorial head bobbing, talking. That, and there is that backyard rooster of theirs crowing anytime day or night, for no apparent reason—crowing whenever it wants, as loud and as long as it wants because, maybe, he was there first, before anything like a university. The Filipino nurses, their shift done and, on their way to catch the bus, will sometimes stop, peer through the gate and make clucking sounds. But the rooster knows a ruse when it hears one, and never answers.

In the bathroom still hangs the notice "Don't place tissues in the toilets.". At first, what seems so many years ago now, I thought that can't be right—a cultural misunderstanding, something lost in translation—but no, they meant it, and to prove it someone had neatly placed a plastic pink container in the corner, an arrow pointing: Tissues Go Here. Regardless of all the signs, warnings and arrows, I couldn't believe they really and truly meant it, but they did and for days the pipes would be clogged, the bathroom closed for maintenance. After four years somebody somewhere finally found the money to make the pipes larger, and now all is well, but not so fast because just the other day I decided to peel off one of the no-longer-needed Tissues Go Here signs, placing it neatly into the garbage. Next day it was back on the wall, the words in bold, fire-engine red.

There is an email from Ahmad that cryptically reads: "Feeling much better, thanks for asking." This does not sound like the Ahmad I know and when I read it again, it still does not sound like him. The other emails are a wasteland of advertisements, football scores, an assessment committee trolling for members.

That night I call Ahmad to ask him how he is feeling. "How are you feeling?"

He is slow in answering but when he does it sounds weak and untested. "Ok, I think. How about yourself?"

"I am good . . . good."

He attempts to spark a conversation about classes and students and even assessment, but I will have none of it, and say, "Good night."

I can envision Ahmad at home, in front of the TV, feet up on the coffee table, sockless, the mandatory stack of student papers by his side, and when the telephone rings he hurries to slip on his sandals, to give his hair a quick combing. Ahmad at home with telephone and TV and his slow-healing surgery that is gradually making him a new and better man.

The dean sends an email reminding all about the rules and regulations of test-taking. Yesterday in front of the library, a student flipped his still-smoking cigarette at my feet, and when I stopped to stare, he said sorry, didn't see me, etc. I put a foot on its smoldering, crushing it into the pavement, moving on, hearing what sounded like muffled laughter, but I could be wrong.

Diner Charles makes me one of his extra special cheeseburgers. That's what he says, 'extra special', with a wink and a nod. He turns his back to me to make it extra special, and when he hands it over, neatly wrapped, it feels richly heavy. On to the fifth floor, door locked, I unwrap a cheeseburger that is stuffed with onions and lettuce. I think we have different ideas about extra special—Charles and me.

Not long after that, no longer hungry and the door unlocked, John walks in like it's more his office than mine, and when I say, "Good afternoon," he answers, "Think so?"

I wait through two lungful sighs before asking, "What?"

"It's happening again."

"It is?"

"Yes, there was the one and like always, others will follow. Of course."

I think about asking him about The Song of Roland, if he can sing it, but instead blurt out, "How about that Beowulf. Some hero, heh?"

The glare of Grendel.

"Ok, what are we talking about, John?"

"I sense another grade appeal on the horizon, that's what. Can you imagine, after all these years and now back-to-back grade appeals. It's a damn shame, that's what it is, damn shame. Criminal . . ."

I hold up my traffic cop hand that almost never works anymore. "John, nothing's finalized yet, we haven't even started final exams."

Showing me a traffic cop hand of his own, "Never mind that, it's coming I tell you, as sure as rain, it's coming."

His rain simile does not work since we live in the middle of a desert, and I almost call him on it but, on second thought, wisely stay quiet. As if rehearsed, we both turn to look out the window, at the Gulf. I have to look twice because there are no ships. That has never happened—a shipless Gulf—and when I turn to report this to John, to maybe grab hold of his arm, he is gone.

The other day I started doing something that I have never done before: when I talk to people, I touch their arm, wrist, hand—anything with flesh on it. This is not a good idea, and I don't know why I am doing it except strangely it does not feel as wrong as I know it should.

Shortly after John had come and gone, I see Marshall in the hallway, reading the newspaper. I startle him with a "Hello", placing a hand on a dragoned elbow, asking, "How's everything going?"

He looks at his elbow as if I might have smudged his tattoo, blurred a dragon claw. "Ok, things are fine," he answers suspiciously.

"Good, very good," and I move away, wondering why 'very'. I can feel him watching me, a fresh heat on the back of my neck.

"It won't be long now, Martin. It's coming, you know," he says. I have no idea what he is talking about but when I stop to look back, he is grinning, turning the pages of his newspaper and grinning. "Martin, have a nice day."

Someone somewhere is playing *You Ain't Nothing But a Hound Dog*, and when I stop to listen, it stops too. I wait for it to return, and it does, only softer. I step into the hallway and yes, as suspected, it is coming from the Spanish adjuncts' office. The song plays five or six times, and in between there are giggles and *Oles*. The Spanish adjuncts are young, fearless and important; I wonder if I'm the only one who is aware of this, who even thinks of them as being important. Before the day is done, John sends me an official memo complaining about the noise, about their disrupting his morning preparation time, etc. I respond with an official "Noted."

That night I dream about Marshall and his unspoken adventure in jail. It is more muddy than bloody.

ﻋﻋﻋ

"The Ministry of Education is stopping by next week, you know." The dean has asked me to a private meeting.

"No, I didn't know."

"Yes, and we are asked to be prepared."

"Prepared?"

"Prepared."

"Will I have to wear a suit and tie?"

She doesn't think this is funny, and says so, "That isn't funny, not at all. We must take this seriously. You know that."

"Is there to be a meeting? Many meetings?"

"Not sure."

"Sounds serious."

"Could be. On the other hand they could come and be gone in thirty minutes, or, stay the entire day, interview students, faculty, visit classes, ask to see files, reports, open your desk drawers.'"

"You're joking? About that desk drawers' part?"

"Maybe." Shrugging a shrug that says 'yes', I want it to be a joke, and yet?

Later that day I send an email to the department, alerting

them to the Ministry coming sometime next week, to be on their toes, and, perhaps, to expect visitors in their classrooms. This last part, I know, is especially sensitive and almost immediately I get urgent return emails from Sara and Marshall, both double daring the Ministry to come anytime they want, but, reminding me that what they see is what they get.

I respond with a, "Noted."

ॐॐॐ

There is a face at the door and at first, I don't recognize it because it is shiny and wet and red. Still, "Hello? Please come in." She enters without saying a word. Along with the shinywetredness, her lips are trembling, and I lean over my desk to peer into the hallway, to see who else might be there, but she is alone.

"Nouf?" I say as if I need more practice recognizing students with shiny, redwet faces.

"Yes, it's me."

"Yes, it is. Nouf, what's wrong?" I motion for her to take a chair. The redness glistens over her cheeks, a small snail of snot peeking from one nostril.

"Nouf?"

"Yes sir." I place a box of tissue in front of her.

"Sir? May I shut the door?"

I get out of my chair and click the office door shut. As a rule this shutting the door is a terrible idea but this helps and she wipes her face clean. When she is ready, she takes a deep breath, and "It's my grade, sir. My grade for the course."

"It is?"

"My grade."

She is not interested in looking at me but at her fingers coiled pink and animal-like resting in her lap, fingernails chewed to the quick.

I watch her watch her fingers, until "Yes, you are not doing well. You are not doing well at all. Missing too many classes, late and incomplete assignments. We have spoken about this more than once. So yes, I remember well."

"Well. . ." looking down into her finger-coiled lap. "Well, my parents are not happy."

I lean back in my chair relieved that it is only that, disgruntled parents. I sigh. "Yes, I can imagine. Parents can be like that."

Nouf likes to sit as far to the right in the classroom as she can get, next to the wall, where she can easily recharge her cellphone. Nouf has one of those looks: although she may be looking directly at me, nodding at all the right times, I know she is looking and nodding at something else, something that has nothing to do with me, the class.

"Sir, my father is especially unhappy with my grade." We both wait for something more, and finally, "My father is very strict about things like this. . . grades—always has been, you know."

Although I don't know, I say yes anyway.

Her eyes slowly move away from her lap, as she surveys my desktop: assorted books, papers, a file labeled Quiz One, a coffee cup half full of yesterday's cold Diner coffee.

"My mom too, but in a different way, but Dad first and foremost, can I say that 'first and foremost'?"

"Yes, that will do."

Her tears have stopped, now only red-rimmed eyes, along with blotchy cheeks, like she just walked in out of a snowy day. That is when she slowly lifts the sleeves of her blouse, pushing them past her elbows. "See this?"

At first, I can only think that her arms are dirty, or no, a squiggle of henna, there seems to be a pattern. But looking closer, squinting, I see it is something else, bruises, strips of greenbrown bruises that start at her forearms, snake up to her elbows, and disappear into the white of her blouse.

My mouth works fishlike. I look at her face, at her bruises, back to her face. "What happened?"

It is as if we are taking a journey, Nouf and I, starting with a wetred face at the door, to sitting, to shutting the door, to tissue, to listening, and now this; we are nearing our destination. "What happened?" This brings back the tears, but nothing like sobbing, just tears draining in straight lines down her cheeks. She whispers something and I lean closer, "What? One more time."

"My dad…"

Looking back at the bruises on her arms, staring at them as if they were something bigger, more important than. . . I fight the urge to reach, to touch the greenbrown flesh, as if seeing weren't enough.

"My dad," she says, now looking at me for the first time, "my dad says if you don't give me a passing grade, the grade he paid for, he will hit me again and again. This is what he says, my dad. He will keep hitting me until the grade is made right. He says it is up to you, Professor."

The snail of snot has found its way back to her nostril, and looking down at my clenched-white fists that have somehow moved to the desktop, she whispers, "I am so sorry, Professor, so very sorry."

ॐॐॐ

There is no wind today, not even one of those sandy whispers, and for some reason that only seems right. A windless day. When the telephone rings my hand twitches, as if ringing and twitching hands are in some mysterious Pavlovian way connected. I let it ring twice and on the third ring, as I reach to pick it up, it stops. I squint to see who it can be, it is a number I don't recognize. This starts me thinking about other near misses, but nothing comes to mind. Instead of near misses I think of women walking in high heels. I am having a hard time making connections today; relationships refuse to logically align. If I smoked, I would pull out a cigarette, light it and puff. If I smoked.

That night the electricity goes out, and although it is not that hot, barely warm, the moment the house goes dark I break out in a sweat. There must be a psychological term for this, but sitting in the dark in the middle of the night, I can't imagine what it would be. Sometimes it is a simple hiccup in the system—wrong switch thrown, buttons gone unpressed, someone forgetting to do his job—and almost immediately all flickers back to bright. But not this time. I fumble through drawers and closets looking for candles but find nothing. This is when she reminds me that we need to be better prepared for things like this. I say she is right, and next time will get it right, but until then we bump into chairs and tables as we worm our way from room to room to room. Luckily, the girls are asleep or there would be more bumping, squeals, the double-darkness breeding beasts of all sorts. When I look out the window to see how far the blackout stretches, the mosque two streets over are lit. I think that if I sit and sweat long enough I will, eventually, grow weary and stumble off into the blackness of the bedroom that I know is thataway. But until then… I can only stare at the electricity that works at the mosque two streets over.

Sometime in the gray of early morning, the lights click on, waking us up. It is my job to walk through the house, turning lights off. In the end, I return to bed and lay awake, waiting for the bigger, brighter morning to arrive. And the Spring Break is over.

The storage room is two doors down from Reedah's office. For a storage room that is full of books and papers and cameras and pens and pencils that should be locked, it almost never is, and I take advantage of this to go there, and carefully looking both ways to see that the coast is clear, quietly slip in, snapping the door tight behind me.

I sit on a box of copy machine paper and survey the shelves in front of me. The top shelf is for the cameras that seven years ago used to be state of the art but are no longer, but never mind, they still work, sometimes. A neat row of big-eyed cameras looking down at me. The second shelf is dedicated to an assortment of other media equipment: microphones, batteries, endless colorful wires that, if plugged in the right way, are useful. At the end of the shelf sits the mysterious teleprompter that we have never used, will never use, but is there, just in case, boxy and unopened. The bottom shelf is booklets and boxes of red pens, blue pens, black pens, magic markers, erasers, paperclips. Except for the bathrooms, the storage room is the darkest, coolest cubicle in the building and I sit scanning the shelves until I hear voices in the hallway. When that happens, I stand up and step to the shelves as if I am searching for something, running my fingers over the tightly packaged teleprompter. But the voices come and go, and for the time being I can return to my box of paper. Once, not too long ago, Reedah, opened the door, switched on the lights while I was sitting there. Her look was anything but surprise, and even though I said Hi, she grabbed a box of blue pens, responding with, "It figures."

Before I could let her go, I asked, "I thought we always kept this room locked. Store room you know. Should keep it locked to keep the riffraff out. Anybody could waltz in and take whatever they want. If they do that there goes the budget, *sah?*"

Cradling her box of blue pens, she sighs, "Usually it is locked, and I have the key. So what are you saying?"

"Oh no, I am not out to reprimand you. Heavens no. I was just wondering, that's all. Wondering." And I stand to let her know that we are finished.

"Yes, well, I will lock it now if that's ok with you. By the way, were you looking for something, something I can help you find?"

Of course this is her way of joking, of showing me she knows what I am all about, and to prove it she smirks.

"Nope, nothing really. Just, just, counting to see how many boxes of paper we have left."

My laugh lacks conviction, which leads her to say, "There are four boxes left, and you were sitting on two of them." And with that she turns off the light, clicking the door shut as she leaves.

The next week I will try the storage room again, and this time it will be properly locked, but the week after that it won't be and I will go in, find my box of printing paper, sit and listen to the hum of the department move about me.

恃恃恃

Two familiar faces are at the door, smiling. I have seen these two girls around campus for what seems like years, and if we share an elevator, they will say Good Morning, How are you, and I will say Morning and fine, and after a short silence, ask them, "How are classes this semester?" This, for some reason, always excites them, and not knowing any different they tell me, in agonizing detail, how their classes are. And now here they are, at my door, grinning.

"Hello."

"Hello. Everything ok? How are classes going?"

But today they are not interested in this and tell me so. "Quite frankly professor, we aren't interested in that but we just dropped by to say Happy Birthday. As you might know, although we have never taken a class with you, you are our favorite teacher."

The quiet one blushes, the other, the speaker, not. She is eager for more.

"Well, that is very flattering, but I am afraid it's not my birthday."

"Well of course it is," says the talker, the other growing redder, cracking her knuckles.

"No, there is some mistake. My birthday isn't for another three months."

"But we brought you a present, Miya and me, see." They pull a box of chocolate from a plastic bag, chocolate with a bright blue ribbon. "So you see, it is your birthday after all."

The blusher, done cracking her knuckles, looks at me for the first time, but her smile is gone.

"This is very kind of you, really, but it isn't…"

"Yes, well never mind that, somebody said it was and we believed them and here we are and here is the present and it no longer matters, Happy Birthday."

I look at the blusher, saying, "Miya, is it?"

Her eyes grow wide and she nods.

"Miya, I want to thank you for the present. It was very generous of you, both of you, and I promise to enjoy your gift."

They are done, and as she stuffs the now-empty plastic bag into her purse, the nameless talker ends with, "You sure have a lot of books in your office. Have you read all of them?"

I haven't but say, "Yes, in a way it's my job."

This sends Miya back to cracking her knuckles, and I think there can only be so much cracking at one time per knuckle and surely she has used up her quota for the three or four minutes they have been in my office. As a finale they end with a "We have missed you, professor." For some reason, somewhere, someone has taught them to say things like this as a sign of respect, or politeness. She means well but the hollowness of such a sentence brings tears to my eyes. She sees this, they both do, and I can only imagine they believe the tears are for something else. "*Wallah*, we miss you."

Once they leave, waving good-bye, I place the box of chocolates in my top drawer. When I do, I quickly think of the Ministry that will be here next week and what they might say, do, if they open my desk drawer and discover gift-wrapped chocolates. I take the box out of the drawer and walk down to Reedah's office. She is on the telephone and when she sees me, she holds the telephone to her chest, saying, "Yes?" I hand the box to her. "Here. For you and your family."

"What's this for?"

"From me to you. I can do that if I want, right?"

"Students gave this to you, didn't they?"

"Does it matter? I want you to have it. A gift from me to you for your birthday."

"It's not my birthday, you know that."

"It isn't?"

She quickly takes the chocolate, wedges it in her purse and goes back to talking on the telephone.

I walk out but then almost immediately return, asking, "Who are you talking to?"

Telephone back against her chest. "What?"

"Who's on the phone?"

"Really, Professor Martin? Really?"

"No, not really. In fact never mind, still Happy Birthday."

"Good-bye."

"If you need me, I'll be in my office, you know. If you need me. In fact, if anybody needs me, I will be in my office. In fact, I will be in my office even if nobody needs me."

"Good-bye, Mr. Chair."

❧❧❧

A mother with two children along with purple-pajamaed maid are waiting at my door. She is carrying the daughter—tiny hands clamped firmly around her neck—while the maid holds the boy's hand. All are quiet, watchful, standing soldierly.

"Hello, Professor."

"Hello."

"Professor, I am so sorry but today is not working for me," and she motions to her children with maid. "How do you say, it has been one of those days. In fact, it's bigger than just one day, and that's why I'm here." Tiny daughter hands feverishly working her neck, pulling at her earlobes.

The maid with boy smiles.

"Quite alright. The best-laid plans of mice and men… Not to worry."

The daughter has yet to show her face, the boy burying his head deeper into the maid's purple-pajamaed leg.

"Please come in."

As a unit they shuffle in, and as if moving from hallway to office is a signal, the children begin to whimper. The maid's shh-hhhing helps. As I find my chair, I think whatever it is she wants, needs, is taking far too long to materialize.

"Professor, it is not complicated, believe it or not, my situation; it is just that nothing has gone right this term, you see, , ." with more motioning towards her children with maid. Now she hands the daughter to the maid, the girl squirmy and unhappy with being detached.

"Although the deadline to withdraw from classes is past—two weeks ago I think—I desperately need to withdraw from Dr. John's writing class, because,"…for a third time motioning to children with maid that have now moved behind her… "because what Dr. John is asking of me is not possible, I know that now. Not possible. Others can do it if they don't have children, a family, but for the rest of us… Well, it can't be done, you see. Simply out of the question. So please help me with this late withdrawal."

"But the term is over?"

"Please."

"But the term is over."

"Please."

By now there are tears and I turn to hand her a tissue. The children, hearing her new teary voice, begin to whimper, and only after much shhhhing by the maid do they stop, the tears, like Mom, glistening in their eyes.

This is when the maid, who is crawly with children, says, "Yes, please help us, please, sir."

All four of us stop to look at her, the mother holding the tissue at her nose, the children open-mouthed like chicks.

The maid says it again, "Please help us."

For some reason this has made the issue doubly serious, and I surprise myself by saying, "Yes, I will look into it. I might be able to help."

"Really? Truly?"

The tears disappear and while the daughter is happily reattached to her mother's neck, the little boy has started to pull at the papers on my desk, his fingers inching toward a pile of silvery paperclips. I look one last time at the maid who will not meet my gaze, not now.

Only later, after they thank me and leave, will I realize that I have no right saying this, that, in fact, there is very little I can do to help. But it's not my fault, the Indonesian maid made me do it.

❧❧❧

Walking to campus today I watch a cat cross the road. It does it in uncertain fits: starting then stopping, backing up, no, going forward, until finally hurling itself across the car-infested street in a daring, uncatty way. A city bus roars by its windy backwash pushing the cat to the curb. Quickly it rights itself, glances to see who saw and hurries off. All of this takes me back, to a day last year, during the middle of the holy month of Ramadan. Rubbing my palms on my pants, as I think back. . . .A trio of neony red-vested street workers is digging a hole to repair a sewage pipe that sprang a terrible leak, not to mention stench; and now, while others are hurrying to be with friends and family for *Iftar*, the three of them wallow knee-deep in the muck of a late Ramadan afternoon. With handkerchief over my nose, I stop to listen, to watch them, hearing the suckmuck of their rubber boots; and of course traffic has slowed and now somebody has decided to honk, followed by yelling, demanding that others go faster, that can't you see it's almost *Iftar*, and that for God's sake let them do their road work some other time, any time but now, with *Iftar* only eighteen minutes away. Get out of the way. It is overcast, making the day look cold, or at least cool, but of course it is not, and looking down, hands in pockets, there is a mound of rubble and dirt and rocks from the hole, and at first, I think it is nothing more than a wad of blueblack garbage that, like always, has been left for someone else to pick up, but as I move closer, I see it is a mangled ball of dead kitten. I stop to look. This shredded no name body curled in the dirt, its tail broken L-shaped, a chunk of fur ripped away, leaving a swathe of pink kitten skin. I squat to see, and yes, there is a patch of black fur, a once-red tongue aaahing, teeming with ants. Flies drink from its eyes. As the workers hurry to repair the sewage pipe, bigger and louder honkings surrounding them, it is just the two of us near that mound of dirt and muck, dead kitten, and me. I touch it with the toe of my shoe. It is still fresh-dead soft and what I think is its belly curls to meet my toe. For the smallest moment, the ants scurry, the flies jump up. The loss of one mangled no-nothing kitten in a city full of thousands of cats, dogs, birds, people is nothing? As two of the red-vested diggers yell to get the ruined pipe out and the new one in, I kick some of the loose dirt and pebbles onto its broken body, covering what I can, as if that will make a difference. Their shiny new sewer pipe in, the workers slowly climb out of their hole to stomp the mud and muck from their boots. While the *Iftar* rush continues, people impatient and angry to get home before the sun sets, I too walk on, a sorrow washing over me that has nothing and everything to do with the death of one unimportant kitten—no more than a handful of once-life—there looms the disappearance that awaits us. And what do I do? I step back onto the sidewalk and think about cancelling classes, calling in sick. Others do it all the time, why can't I? During the holy month of Ramadan, with *Iftar* only moments away…Later, by the time I reach my building, my fifth floor, my office, the urge to cancel my day, my classes, and go home is forgotten; only later that afternoon will I recall my dead-kitten sadness and wonder what the fuss was all about.

ىف ىف ىف

Hala is not a bad student, just ask the person who writes her papers for her. At first, I gave her the benefit of the doubt, although I recall I did, one day, pose the question to her: "This is your work, isn't it? Hala, your words, and not somebody else's, right?"

"Oh yes, absolutely, sir. All my ideas, my thoughts, for sure."

Although that wasn't what I had asked, I smiled and nodded, as if it were close enough.

Then, she did it again with the next paper, only better; and so, "Hala, you did it again, only better."

I wait for her to take this into a meaningful direction. "What do you mean?"

"Hala, are you bipolar?"

"What is that?"

"Hala, quite simply you're in-class writing is nothing like your out-of-class writing. In fact, they are two completely different styles: one excellent, the other not. How is that?"

Hala is tall and lean, and sometimes wears an *abaya*, sometimes not. Today is a non-*abaya* day. Her eyebrows are dark and perfectly rectangular, and when she frowns there is a nearness about her that makes me look down at my hands.

"Sir, I can answer that. You see, when I have time to think, to put my thoughts together, I do much better. But give me only fifty minutes, and I flounder. Know what I mean? Flounder?"

I like the word flounder but it all smacks of a well-rehearsed speech, and I wait for her to go on, but this is as far as she has practiced. Smiling still, I move on to step two: we go over some of the words and phrasing of her paper, and when I point to words like, 'homophobic' and 'imperative', asking her what they mean, she answers with, "I am not sure, but I know the Arabic."

I let the silence linger. Before she leaves, she stops at the door, announcing, "Professor, I am an engineering major, you know, computer engineering, and this writing of English, these essays that everybody wants us to do is no good in engineering. Numbers, formulas, physics is what I am all about. This English is getting in my way, can you understand? In my way and putting me behind schedule."

Later, she hands in her best paper yet—the stuff of graduate school.

"Hala, enough. This is not your work, your writing, your English on these pages."

Today is an *abaya* day, and when I ask her to take a seat she does not. "But like I told you before, these are all my ideas, my thoughts," motioning to her paper that I have stretched out before us on the desktop like some skinned animal.

"Hala, stop. You are cheating. Somebody else is writing your papers. This is cheating."

It is too easy to be angry with her and I fight back the urge but the longer she denies the obvious, the more impatient I become. Like some lawyer, all I want is a confession.

9

Thomas has had a heart attack. They just moved him from the clinic to the hospital. When I call him, he sounds surprisingly himself, saying, "It's not serious, but just to be sure they've carted me here. That's what the doctors say, "Just to be sure, safe.' They wheelchaired me through the doors, up the elevator, to here." I close my eyes to listen and when I do, I can see his nose hairs twitching, his eyes a weary watery red. The department will send him flowers, a get-well card, but Thomas will not read the card; he will give the flowers to nurses, the x-ray technician. "Martin, I have to go, the nurse is here to give me my medicine, to make sure I swallow it— imagine. Two of the largest purple pills you've ever seen, or maybe not." And he hangs up. I open my eyes and check the schedule to see who can take his classes for the rest of the week. This is the first time he has ever called me Martin.

Students are happy as the end of the term nears. For me, there are department reports to write, something to do with assessment and reaccreditation policies has reared its ugly head, and I must sit and write faculty evaluations for all, even heart-tired Thomas. That, and my office windows are extra dirty, but there is no way to clean them from the outside unless they rent one of those cranes or lower one of the willing, or not, Egyptian workers from the roof, with spray bottle and squeegee in hand. Every now and again, I see some pink-pajamaed maid leaning out of a tenth- floor apartment window, stretching to wipe the glass clean, spray bottle in one hand, rag in the other. Sometimes these maids go too far, step out onto a narrow dusty ledge that was never meant for bare feet, slip and tumble to their death. The newspapers might report it as a suicide (*Disgruntled Maid Jumps to Her Death*) while others will know it for what it is: a maid leaning too far to get that one last smudge from the glass. My windows will remain dirty.

Here they come again, their shift over, two brightly colored gangs of nurses from the hospital next door. The first group is Indian, in blue and purple garb; they are loud, laughing, and sometimes walk hand-and-hand. Not far behind them are the Filipino nurses dressed in white; they are not as loud, but even from the fifth floor I can hear them singing. We use the next-door hospital as a selling point for recruiting faculty: "In addition, we have one of the best hospitals in the city right next door to the campus, no more than a three-minute walk, and beyond that, perhaps another five-minute walk, is a McDonalds." I watch the two groups, in no real hurry, even slowing to make sure the others catch up, to retell a joke, to share a song. Regardless, everything is funny. One of them goes to the fence to serenade the neighbor's rooster, who, of course, will have none of it. I think of Thomas and his heart, and try hard to feel sorry for him, but nothing comes. In no time the nurses are at the bus stop, arm-in-arm, hand-in-hand, waiting for their busses. I try one last time with Thomas but nothing—just a portrait of Tom with nostrils all wrong.

୭ଚ୭

Students are arguing in the hallway, and I give them a chance to solve things by themselves but when it continues, even growing louder—something like a snarl from one of them—I step out to see. There are two boys, maybe 13 or 14 years old, and I want to believe they are lost, entered the wrong building—the football field is two streets over. They simply offer me a glance—an adult has stepped into the hallway—and go back to being loud. Finally, I ask them, "Is everything alright here?"

They stop long enough to glance at me before continuing, this time using their hands, their fingertips, to show how impatient they are with one another. I consider this until, "Please shut up."

They look at me as if to say, 'Why didn't we think of that?'

"Shut up. You know the words?"

What can only be the older of the two, a pimply forehead and more braces than teeth, says, "Oh yes, we know these words, thank you."

"Good. Can I help solve your loudness in front of my door?"

This is when the other, younger, turns to get a good look at me; his pants don't fit and his belt has missed two belt loops. "Can you help us?"

This is becoming complicated when all I seek is quiet, and so, sensing that we have reached some sort of agreement, say, "Ok. Thank you, just shut up."

The older one, whose pimples have suddenly turned angrier, redder, smiles, "Just shut your door. If we are too loud, just shut your door."

The baggy pants one grins at this solution. I am not sure how angry I should be with grinning all around. Thinking of Thomas and his almost-heart attack, of nurses joyfully walking past to get to their busses to go home, to eat dinner, to wash their clothes and maybe call their families in Manila and New Delhi, I do as told and softly shut my door, and when I do their argument ends, as they move down the hall.

⋙⋙⋙

I sense the lovers are no more. He has not shown himself for weeks, while she continues, her desk aimed straight ahead, a hint of a smile. Since his absence, she has morphed into somebody else: she asks questions, answers questions; she is no longer fearful of reading when I call for volunteers. After class, on Wednesday, I ask, "Dina, please see me before you leave."

"Am I in trouble? If I am I didn't mean it, I really didn't."

"No, no, nothing like that. But before you leave."

Later, the classroom is empty except for the two of us. "Just curious, but is everything alright with you these days?"

"Yes, why do you ask?"

"No reason, except you have changed, for the better, I think, and I haven't seen your partner, Tarek, is it, for quite some time."

"You are asking me if I am alright or if Tarek is alright?"

This catches me off guard, but she helps me with, "Professor, I am very fine, thank you. Very fine. And Tarek might be fine, too, but I'm not sure."

"Just curious. None of my business. Curious."

She considers this for a moment, before asking, "Will that be all, Professor? It's good to hear I'm not in trouble."

"Yes, yes, just curious."

With the fall term a summer away, she comes up to me and says she isn't registered for the class, says she knows I said there were no more seats available but she would really like to join my class in the fall, if that is at all possible and even if there isn't enough room she doesn't mind, not really, sitting on the floor, if that's ok with me, and…Her piece of jade is bigger, greener, her hair wispy, and nothing like Nasreen's. Now that she is done talking, and since I haven't said a thing, she looks down, thinking that silence must be the same as no. But I am looking at her dirty green shard of jade, the way it is caught in the scoop of her throat, lazing there on its side, resting. And so I take out my pen, and ask, "What is your name?"

She smiles, "My name is Noura, and . . ."

␚␚␚

Grade-appealer Maryam enters my office, asking, "How are you, Professor?"

"I am ok, Maryam. Ok."

"Just ok, is it? Isn't that about a C grade? Just ok? Average?"

For some reason I am willing to play with her on this morning, and so, "Yes, I feel C today. However, later, you never know, my ok could become a good, or even a great."

"Good is a B?"

"Sure a B. But never mind, can I help you with something, Maryam?"

Fingers to her lips, she considers the question as if it were a trick, after all we are playing. Finally, "Not today, no thank you. Good-bye, Professor."

I end up staring at the spot where she stood, blinking, feeling strangely used, like some *bakalah* man, selling cigarettes, candy, milk, bottles of water, and she came in to window shop but finding nothing worth her time or money, leaves empty-handed.

When I hear the dean's high heels coming down the hallway, my way, I look for a place to hide. But my office is small, cluttered, and the only real possibility is to squeeze behind the open door. Her high heels moving closer, louder, almost here, and so I wedge myself behind the door. I hear her stop at the door, look in, and seeing my chair is empty, her high heels turn and go back the way they came. I stay where I am and think about what I would have said if she had discovered me behind the door. *Just looking at the hinges, you know. Door needs a repainting, too. Hinges replaced and a new paint job. Somebody's got to look for these things. Somebody, don't you think?*

❧❧❧

I admit that over the years I'd given it some thought, but come to think of it, it was more the stuff of fantasy than anything else. But never mind, because now, with the term coming to an end, I've decided it's as good a time as any. Like always, I start by stepping up to the podium. For today's class I have brought only one page of notes, a single sheet of yellow legal paper, and even that is more paper than notes. With one finger I slide the paper from one side of the podium to the other, then back again. Two ceiling lights at the back of the classroom are missing. Meanwhile a sort of mid-morning hush falls over the class, but not for long as somewhere towards the back, near the windows, someone, almost certainly Yousef, whispers unafraid, "Welcome, Professor, welcome," followed by a tiny flurry of classmate giggle.

"Yes, well, before we start today please indulge me for just a moment, if you don't mind, as I remind you about something. I promise you this won't take long." There is a general shuffling of feet, a shifting of chairs, as Yousef, yet again, says something, which only those in the back can hear and think funny. I smile even though I try not to, then take a deep breath, as if to demonstrate: this is what you do before putting your head underwater.

"Yes, well, as you know, or maybe not, for many years I have been a professor of English but, I have always had a keen interest in history, specifically American History, more specifically yet twentieth-century American history, and to go one step further, America's involvement in World War Two."

At this point, Rawan, who is never late, walks in late, opening the classroom door spy-like, peeking in, saying, "Sorry to be late," scurrying to find a front row seat, before saying, one last time, "So sorry." From the back is Yousef, assuring her, "It's quite all right. No problem." There is laughter, but not much.

The classroom fidgeting all done, I readied myself, looking down at the one page. "Yes, well, so it's been established that I am, among other things, all about American history and World War Two, and to prove it, allow me to remind you that I have written a handful of scholarly articles on the subject; as a matter of fact, I even won a prize for one of them, six years ago. Granted, it was not much of a prize: two-hundred dollars along with a piece of paper that said good for me, but never mind because an award is an award, right?" The award part was not something I had meant to say, not in the notes; in fact, it never even crossed my mind, but once I started, it seemed like a natural fit. I look down at my one yellow page.

It is then, as if rehearsed, that a general classroom malaise trickles through the class: a yawn, a sigh, an assortment of glances at the clock on the wall, vacant stares out the window, looking into the trees across the street, watching birds, and so on. I see all but glancing down at my one page I continue. "And so, today I am here to tell you—and you may very well be some of the first to learn this—that after all these years and after thorough research, study and investigation, we now know that it was not the Japanese who bombed Pearl Harbor, oh no, not those Japanese, but in fact it was the Chinese."

All classroom busyness abruptly stops, replaced by much looking straight at me, the World War Two expert in the front of the room. There is silence. There is blinking. No Yousef, no backrow chatter. When Rawan softly takes out her notebook and begins writing, some of the others follow her lead. As the quiet holds, the wall clock takes on a new tick-tock bigness. I wait, take the yellow page and fold it once, twice and slip it into my pocket. I wait one more time just to be sure, placing both hands on the podium, until finally I take another deep breath, walk out the door and into the hallway.

I'd never given it much thought until now, but once by myself in the hallway, I take a long, hard look, and it is a normal college hallway: a neatly polished bowling-alley long floor, with bulletin boards attached here and of course a door, and another door and another, and … the walls are painted a soft hospital green. I can hear Yousef's voice, but when it finishes there is nothing like laughter. Folding my arms like I am waiting for a bus, leaning against the wall, I am in no hurry to reenter the classroom. In fact, according to my pocketed notes, I am to count slowly to twenty-five before going back to the podium to take a look at their faces one more time before setting things straight. But at fifteen, the door opens and out steps Yousef with backpack on his shoulder, and before I can say anything, make any sort of announcement, Yousef asks, "If we are done for the day, can we go?"

Final exam time has arrived, and there is an outbreak of end-of-semester worry. Students can't believe that the end has come so quickly, that, come to find out, they are not passing the class, and, come to think of it, that is unfair because the professor never once notified them that they were failing—not once—and 'how are we supposed to know; and oh, by the way, we've missed too many classes and this too smacks of unfairness because he never warned us, never said a word about this attendance stuff. How unfair is that, *sah?*' Like every semester. I am prepared, with copies of the grade appeal form stacked neatly on the corner of my desk.

For two and a half days my telephone does not ring, the emails are dull, nobody knocks at my door. I email myself and check with IT to see if the phone is in working order. They ignore my email. I open my door extra wide. Finally I look up when I hear footsteps but nobody walks by. It's as if this part of the hallway is broken, off limits. But then, on day three, just when I am beginning to think this lull is not such a bad idea, the onslaught begins. A line of students is waiting at my office door, and when I good morning them, only one offers me a good morning back.

Even before I can unlock my door, they crowd behind me, talking, . . *"inshallah, . . wallah,"* and when I ask them to wait until I open the door and sit down, they answer with "Take your time," but never stop talking. Five of them crowd into my office, but I only have chairs for two; in the end, only one has something she insists is a complication, the others are moral support, are there to provide storytelling embellishment—if necessary. "To start, he is rude, always has been; not only that he plays favorites, ask anybody in the class." This is when she motions to the others, with one reminding her, "Don't forget the unfair grading. How Noura writes excellent papers, nothing less than an A in high school, and now this. I know, I was there. While there are others in the class who can't write a complete sentence, who cheat, who have others write their papers for them and get better grades, who . . ." I hold up a hand, and this seems to make a difference, and at least for the time being they fall quiet.

I know they are waiting for me to ask who the he is, but it really doesn't matter, and so, "Have you spoken to your professor about any of this?"

"Oh no," she says, the others nodding in silent agreement. "Oh no, how can I? He holds my grade in his hands, this professor. I am completely at his mercy. Completely." Nodding all around.

It is all too much, this early in the morning, and I point towards the stack of grade appeal forms on my desk. "Well, you know if you feel you have been graded unfairly, you can always file a grade appeal."

As one, as if rehearsed, they click their tongues, "*Lah, lah*; we know all about this grade appeal process, how it works, or doesn't; all grade appeals are denied. Teachers must stick together. We know this. Grade appeals are a waste of time and energy, and . . ."

This time when I hold up a hand, they continue to talk through it, as if I am only good for one raised hand per visit.

By now, their case made, their displeasure noted, they grow restless, fingering their cellphones. Sensing the end is near, I ask what I always ask, a question that takes them by surprise, "And what exactly would you like for me to do?"

As they glance at one another, there is a flurry of Arabic

as they back and forth an answer. Noura, the primary figure of unhappiness, has an angry pimple in the center of her chin, and try as she may to cover it up, its big redwhiteness will not be denied. The other four have clear, girly smooth chins.

"Don't know. But there must be something, a policy or procedure, because this cannot stand. Cannot."

It is then that Marshall looms up behind them in the hallway. He is wearing what can only be the shortest short-sleeve shirt he owns, allowing his dragons plenty of room, and when he folds his arms across his chest, the five of them stop, look straight ahead, whisper— the smallest hint of a cower ripples through the office. I fight back an unprofessional smirk.

છ૭છ૭છ૭

Their final papers are due, and I have repeatedly told them that they can drop their papers off in my mailbox, at my office. Three students visit me to discuss their papers, and of course they are the three who least need a visitation. Bedour is one of the three. She tells me she is worried that her 4.0 GPA is in jeopardy, that her scholarship might very well fall apart, that her parents may reconsider her medical school dreams if…

"Not to worry, Bedour. Unless you decide to self-destruct on this paper—and that is not likely—you will do well. There is no reason why you shouldn't."

"You think so, professor? You really think so?"

She says this as if she knows something I don't, as if she is on the threshold of something bigger, more damaging than I can imagine. I watch her face for a hint of sincerity, as she continues to crack her knuckles.

"Yes, Bedour, I do think so," giving her my best I-know-what-I am-talking-about voice.

She has a firm grasp of her paper, scanning, once again, my inky comments. We have gone through it twice, and each time the answers are the same. Finally, with the other two who don't really need to see me at the door, leaning in to hear what they can, she whispers, "Then we are done?"

"Bedour, I dare you to make that into a statement. Go ahead, give it a try."

The other two twitter, bringing a flash of red to Bedour's cheeks. "Ok, we are finished." And with that, her paper triple folded and giving her knuckles one final cracking, she leaves.

The other two want to know if they can come in together, as a unit.

🙝🙝🙝

When I least expects it, Thomas Chapel is at the door, and like always I am surprised to see him and even say so, "Oh, Thomas, you surprised me."

He nods, as if yes, that's the right answer.

Except for brown shoes, Thomas is dressed in black, which makes me believe he doesn't own any black shoes. He stands there as if something is wrong and he is here to make it right. Finally, "Martin, we have to talk."

"Sure. How do you feel?"

"Fine. False alarm, a kind of heart attack but more 'kind' than anything else, but we still have to talk."

"We do?"

"Yes, we need to meet and talk."

"We do?"

"Yes, all of us."

Since his us may not be the same as my us, I wait for more. The laces of his brown shoes are untied, leaning worm-like on the carpet.

"We?"

"Yes," as if I haven't been paying attention. "The department, all of us, even Ahmad."

"Right. Call the meeting, I'm ready."

That's when I realize he is not making a request.

The next morning Peter is waiting for me at my office, and when he sees me, announces, "We have worked out our differences, the editors and me. All is well, I believe, and the book is listed in their fall catalog." In his hand is the catalog, page 33: Peter H. Wilson, *The Milton Mystery Unveiled: Paradise Not Lost.*

He waits for praise and I give it to him. "Well done, Peter."

"Yes. . . well."

"By the way, what's the H for?"

"Sorry?"

"The Peter H…"

"Hinton."

"As in *The Outsiders* Hinton?"

"Very same, thank you."

As I shake his hand, I can't help but secretly wonder how long it has been since Peter shook anybody's hand.

"Yes, well, that's something, hey. Looks like we're almost there. Won't be long."

Peter is done talking, clutching the fall catalog, but I can tell he's having a hard time concluding. He shuffles his un-tied shoe-string feet, glancing at my bookcase, now at the window and the Gulf beyond, until finally, "Nice view."

"Peter, congratulations on the book."

"Yes, . . . well . . ." and that works as a conclusion.

Only later, once he is gone, do I wonder why I didn't tell him about his shoe strings.

❧❧❧

That night it rains loud and hard, like some Malaysian tropical rain forest. The swish against the window puts me to sleep. In the morning, the sidewalks and streets will be bright and clean but not to worry because by noontide the dust will be back and by sunset everything will be back to an exhausted paper bag brown.

"How can I help you?"

"Good morning, Professor."

"Yes, how can I help you?"

"You can't."

"I can't?"

"No." She answers with a big smile that seems to split her face, tearing into her cheeks. I cringe as if it must hurt, something broken, or at least cracked. Her smile holds, even splitting wider.

"Are you ok?" I ask.

"Of course, Professor. Of course."

There is some general waiting, until "I am here to tell you something."

"Yes," I answer. "Many people come to my office for that very thing."

"I am here to tell you that I am very happy with Dr. Peter. In fact, I think he is an amazing professor, even great. I just wanted you to know that."

I move some desktop papers from here to there, and back again. "Sorry, what is your name?"

"Hanan, sir."

"Hanan, did Dr. Peter send you to me?"

Her smile slipping back into her mouth, even beyond, "Oh no, sir. Nothing like that. I am here on my own. Completely by myself."

"I see."

"Yes, I earned an A in his class, and I worked very hard for it, and he even told me I deserved an A, and that's that."

When she holds out her hand, I shake it and she leave, saying, "Sorry to bother you."

For some reason I write down the day and time on a piece of paper. That, and I try smiling like her, showing all my teeth, but I can't, my mouth doesn't work that way.

Later, the embassy sends a message, reminding us to be on the alert, to be watchful of any unusual people or activities in and around town, the campus. There has been talk of terrorist attacks against any and all foreigners. And by the way, stay away from crowds or any political events; this, as we know, can be a magnet for turmoil. Before the day is done the embassy sends this message again, as if the first time wasn't enough, or, more probably, the sender simply forgot he had already sent it.

I go to the window to look down at the campus, at the dusty pathways and almost-green lawns, along with assorted palms. I see no walkers, nothing like students this late in the afternoon. Two taxis have stopped, one in front of the other, warning lights blinking. The two drivers are looking intently at the bumper of the first taxi. The bigger, red-shirted driver holds a telephone to his ear, and with the other hand churns the air in front of him. The smaller driver, who has nothing like a red shirt, leans against his taxi, watching traffic hurry by. Meanwhile, two cats walk side by side in front of the library as if they know something about going to college. They cut across the almost-green grass when suddenly a bird lands nearby. They stop. The bird hops, pecks, hops, pecks, but once it stops hopping and pecking long enough to look up and see its mistake, it blurs away into the trees. The cats restart, even doing something like a catty gallop to rush to the shade. But now something has gone terribly wrong with the two taxi drivers because they have moved to the sidewalk, and the red-shirted one is standing too close to the shorter one, and although I cannot hear them, there is yelling going on, and finally the smaller one is not going to take it anymore and yells back, and now the other decides he has had enough too, giving the smaller driver a mighty shove. He stumbles backwards but rights himself just in time to pull off one of his sandals and wave it at the other's head. It is then, with disrespect filling the air, that another taxi pulls up alongside, and when it does, they stop to look and listen, and as if that is all they needed, hurry back to their taxis, and with one final gesture, slam their doors and drive off. To complete the picture, a blue and white airliner is angling across the Gulf, a smooth effortless slope into the bright air.

ↄↄↄↄↄↄ

When I step out of the elevator a student is waiting for me. We good morning each other and shyly she follows me to my office.

"It's my stomach, sir."

"It is?"

"My stomach."

"Well, you know, I am not that kind of doctor, my mother wanted me to be but, sadly, I have disappointed her."

Rubbing her stomach, she says, "That's something," and then sits down.

"Dr. Marshall says I must take the final exam today, but I can't. You can see that, right? I can't." Rubbing her stomach extra hard, the beginning of watery eyes. "I can't, it's my stomach; I can't think, study. I can't do anything. Can you please help me?"

"You want me to talk with Dr. Marshall about you, for you?"

"If you would—could—he refuses to listen, to care about me. It's not my fault, this stomach business. Not me." Tears finally finding their way down her cheeks.

"When is your final exam?"

"Today, ten-thirty."

"In one hour?"

"Exactly."

With both hands on her stomach, sometimes waist, she is up and at the door, profusely thanking me as she goes.

When I call Marshall, he startles me, answering on the first ring.

"Ah, the chair has come up for air."

"Marshall, you have a final at 10:30?"

For what feels like a very long time, even for Marshall, there is a quiet, until "Yes, I do."

"I just had a student of yours come to see me about some sort of stomach issue, said she couldn't take the test, because of her stomach, etc. Any of that ring a bell?"

"And she asked you to call me?"

"She made a request."

"Who is it?"

I glance at my desk, at the bookcase as if she might have left the residue of a name. "Don't know."

"Never mind, I know who it is."

"You do?"

"Yes, her medical issues are legendary: stomach cramps, headaches, a collection of sprains; just two weeks ago she had something that sounded like leprosy."

"Ok, what do we do?"

"You mean what do I do?"

Like always, Marshall has exhausted me, and I hurry to end the call. "Yes, what do you do?"

"To be realistic, O'chairman, my chairman, it is probably a moot question, and let me tell you why: this young woman of chronic pains and aches is hopelessly failing the course, and whether she sits for the exam or not, is, I believe, irrelevant to all parties concerned. There you have it, as official as I can make it."

The telephone tells me we have spoken for three minutes. "Very good." But then sensing that that is not enough, not for Marshall, I end with, "Carry on."

A snort, followed by, "Roger that."

No sooner do I hang up than the telephone rings; it is the dean calling. I don't answer. Moments later it rings again, this time it is the president's office.

"Morning."

"Yes, it is."

"Pretty early, don't you think?"

"Yes, a student just came by my office complaining about an illness she has and how she can't take a final today and how she spoke to you but you didn't seem keen on helping her, she said. Lots of grabbing at her stomach, this one. Said you could help her, if you wanted to. Said it was wrong for her to be punished for being ill, and if things didn't work out, she would talk to her father, and so on."

"It's one of Marshall's students."

"Is that so. Ok, so I sent her back your way. Said you would take care of her, and, I might add, her father."

"Her father?"

"You know what I am saying? Her father?"

"That important, is he?"

"You said it, I didn't."

When she returns, I tell her not to worry; she can take the final some other time, when she is feeling better.

"I can do that?"

"Yes."

"Dr. Marshall said I could do this?"

"You will take the final once you are better."

She takes both hands away from her stomach to shake my hand.

Over the next couple of days I await a revisit from her, or at the very least a call from Marshall. But there is nothing, and this is both good and bad.

ૐૐૐ

They have decided to set up a traffic checkpoint on the busy street in front of campus. A line of cars and red buses runs from the front gate, through the intersection and beyond. There is the usual check of drivers' licenses, registration, and of course the occasional insistence that the young women drivers share their telephone numbers with them, for the record. There is much honking and flashing of headlights in what has now become a clogged intersection. But the police pay no attention because, after all, there is police work to be done. One of the policeman steps out of his car and moves to the sidewalk to talk to students, laughing. I have seen him before, this one with two silver stars on his uniform shoulders, which I can only imagine allows him unlimited sidewalk time. As he busily shakes hands, our Nepalese security gather at the gate to see the traffic police at work, with real guns.

10

His nametag said 'Early', and in the beginning I had to stop and squint, even re-squint, to make sure I was reading it right. Early? If he was or wasn't, I can't be certain but I do know that he was always there when I arrived.

As a rule, over the years, security people come and go—here one day, gone the next—and every now and again a new company takes charge, which means, of course, new faces, new soldier-like uniforms with golden epaulettes, a broad blue stripe running down the seam of their trousers, like something out of the Bengal Lancers, walkie-talkies that beep and buzz, not to mention that I must show, yet again, my ID card, as they turn it this way and that, holding it up to the light because you never know, until they will shrug, saying, "Thank you, Sir."

But back to Early. In the morning, in the bathroom, I watch him go from sink to sink to sink, letting each faucet run first cold then hot, and then, just for good measure, hold his hand in the water, because when it comes to security you can never be too safe. Once satisfied, he steps to the next sink and faucet and so on down the line. That done, he then goes to the five stalls, flushing each toilet. And yes, I watch as he intently watches each toilet flush properly, frowning into the toilet bowl as the water does its duty before moving on to the next stall. But not so fast, because there is more as he patiently waits, arms folded, hiding his nametag, for each water tank to refill. That done, he then looks to see if there are enough paper towels, to see if the silver hand-blowing machine is in proper blowing order. "Why are these urinals built so high?" I heard him say one day to someone on his walkie-talkie. "Some very tall men must have installed them. Too high for most men, not to mention boys." Taking out a black notebook from his shirt pocket, with ballpoint pen that he clicks to life, he writes. As he heads to the door, he can't help but scan the ceiling, looking at the lights, and sure enough one florescent light is flickering, and so with notebook still firmly in hand, he writes. Before he leaves, he studies the flickering light one last time before sighing and moving on down the hallway, his walkie-talkie crackling.

One morning as he is doing his security check of the 4th floor bathroom, I give him a good morning with handshake and say, "Early, can I ask you one question?"

He smiles and says, "Surely," not surprised that I knew his name because, after all, what are nametags for.

"Well, you are a security guard, right?"

"This is true."

"Yes, well, as security guard why do you feel the need to check the plumbing? I mean, don't we have maintenance for that? It's not your job, Early, this running water and flushing toilets.

Not your job. Security and plumbing are different animals. See what I mean?"

"Animals?" His hands taking a firm grip on his walkie-talkie. "Where? Where are they?"

"Not animals. I mean duties. Different duties."

There is a small pause as he cocks his head to hear his radio crackle. Once the crackle is finished, he smiles, followed by, "Yes sir, you are not wrong but security is security. It is all in the details, don't you think? In fact, excuse me for saying but that is the problem these days, nobody cares a fig for details."

"A fig?"

"Yes sir, a fig. Everybody thinks that being precise is wrong, a waste of time, the faster the better. More flaw than fanfare."

"I like that: more flaw than fanfare. Where did you hear that?"

His hand is once again at his walkie-talkie, fingering the buttons. "My mother is a school teacher. She knows things like this: more flaw than fanfare, thoroughness is a virtue, always be punctual. She is the head teacher for three villages." Now he motions to the row of porcelain sinks with one hand, the line of stalls with the other. "And so, here I am, watching over you, this building, this university, even the country, do you see? And yes, you are entirely welcome."

The very next day, since we are now early-morning friends, Early tells me he owns a degree in psychology. That's what he said, 'own'.

"No, I didn't know that," I say genuinely surprised. "Your

mother must be very proud of you."

"Do you want to see it? The degree? I have a folded copy of it in my wallet." And he starts to pull out his wallet.

"No, no, not necessary. I believe you."

"Yes, but sad to say, who needs a college degree these days?" And he laughs as if it were a joke and I am sure to miss the humor of it but never mind because he will laugh for the both of us. Holding his hands out. "Sir, if truth be told, none of this security requires a college degree, not even a high school diploma."

"Still, you are putting your college degree to work?" I say jokingly. But when he looks at me, I can see there is nothing like fun in his face, more like a grimace.

"Cameras would make it easier, you know."

"Where?"

"Here."

"In the bathroom?"

He shrugs, "Certainly, we all are the same here, in the bathroom."

I think about saying something about his mother, the head teacher of three villages, but decide against it. "All part of being precise, is it?"

He waves a hand that could mean yes, no, why not, don't be silly.

I watch him finish his security check but before leaving he returns to one of the sinks, washes his hands with much soap and lather before pulling out two, three paper towels to dry his hands. Almost out the door now, he leans into his walkie-talkie, declaring, "All clear with 4th floor toilets."

Somebody somewhere answers him with an official "Roger that" crackle.

"And yet you carry a copy of your college degree, just in case? A college graduate guarding the toilets. Well done." It is meant to be funny, a final barb of humor before he goes, but it comes out sounding all wrong, strangely angry.

"Somebody's got to do it, Professor."

"Think so?"

"Absolutely, somebody."

In a feeble attempt to get the last word in, the last noise, the best I can do is click my tongue. When Early turns to look at me one last time, there is a hint of sorrow in his face as if he expected more, something bigger and better, before he lifts the walkie-talkie to his lips, announcing, "Going to the fifth-floor bathroom now."

"Roger that."

As he takes the stairs, I want to apologize but don't.

&‌°&‌°&‌°

It is far too quiet for the end of the term, and sure enough, when Sara sees me walking down the hallway, her direction, she suddenly has the urge to re-enter her office, closing the door behind her. Later, Peter nods a silent good morning. Still later, Reedah stops long enough to give me a doomed doggy-eyed look. I ask, "What?" Reedah is spectacularly indifferent to all that swarms around her; yet she knows all there is to know, and so I try again,

"What?"

Staring into her computer, talking directly into its screen, she replies, "Don't know. You tell me."

I wait for more, but there is only silence as she gazes intently into the screen. When I sigh, she sighs back.

Earlier, in the Diner, Charles, wearing a cartoonishly large, white chef hat, sees me walk in, sees me wave, ignores me and steps into the back room. This morning, the new Nepalese security guard at the gate asked for my ID. I looked through my wallet but couldn't find it. "You know, I have been here for years. Years, and…." But he is new and knows nothing except what he has been told—to check everybody's ID. Relooking through my wallet—unearthing credit cards I didn't even know I owned—a line formed behind me, someone mumbled, "Hurry up." When I turned to look, all eyes were aimed skyward, as if watching the blue of sky was suddenly so important. Finally, I found the ID card with ancient photography, and showed him. He squinted to see the resemblance, turning it this way and that, until "Ok, thank you, sir."

Behind me, "About time."

And so there it is: something is about to happen. With the day almost done, I am at the copy machine when Ahmad comes in, says, Hello and begins copying what appears to be an entire book. I have warned Ahmad about this before; his monthly copying numbers are the highest of us all. My official email memos have gone to him, bringing to his attention that the "Printing/Copying budget is being compromised when you continuously…." He replies with an "Understood." Now this, in plain sight, making no effort to disguise what he is up to. I watch him print, page after page, every now and again tossing something like a smile my direction.

I return to my office to begin a new, more officially threatening email to send him, but by "this blatant abuse of the photocopying policy can no longer be tolerated; as a result, this email will become a portion of your official personal file…" I turn to watch the bluegray crawl of the Gulf at work, with its many ships, the day, like always, a big yellow hot…and delete it all. I am convinced that Ahmad, in his peculiar bow-tied way, knew all along that I would do nothing. This, beyond everything else, disappoints me. So yes, something is coming, approaching, almost here. How does Yeats put it: a slouching headed my direction? I place my head on my hands on my desk to rest.

The next day brings an extra-early heat and by ten o'clock the air conditioning is broken. There is an announcement that maintenance is working on it. "Thank you for your patience and understanding." There are phone calls insisting that the classrooms are too hot, impossible for testing. "Do something about it."

I write back, "Noted."

By 12:30 nothing is fixed and when I ask why, they say it has to do with parts we don't have, but we are waiting for them to be delivered any minute now, it won't be long, in the meantime we are doing all we can. "Thank you for your patience and understanding."

When it comes to air conditioning parts we don't have, there is nothing more to say. Until then, the bathrooms are the coolest places in the building, and when I go there others are standing around washing their hands, looking extra hard and long at themselves in the mirror. I wash my hands, look in the mirror, use paper towels, relook at myself in the mirror, step to the window, and finally, out of bathroom things to do, say good-bye to the others and return to the hallway heat. By 2:30 when the AC is restored the campus is deserted.

That night Peter calls. "It's a done deal."

"It is?"

"Done deal. All agreed. The Milton book will be in my hands by fall. They even used the word 'guaranteed'. Imagine that. So there you have it." We wait and listen to somebody's laughter, somewhere. "Just thought you should know before it's too late."

Before I can ask him about this last part, he says, "*Ciao*," and is gone.

৵৵৵

It is almost bedtime now when the older one needs help with her math. She never uses the word help but simply opens the textbook in front of me, pointing, "What's this problem all about?" When I come up with a right answer, I feel as if a small piece of the day has been salvaged. She snaps the book shut, ending with, "Got it, thanks." When she leaves, the younger one, who should have been in bed hours ago, can't sleep. I tell her to go back to bed and eventually sleep will "consume you."

"What is consume?"

"Take you."

This brings tears to her eyes, and I quickly say, "But it will take you in a good way. The way dreams take you. Like that."

This helps, and the more I talk the more she yawns until finally, "Daddy, I think I am ready to be consumed."

ɢɢɢ

"If I don't pass, I don't graduate. Unfortunately, it's that simple."

I like that he threw in the word unfortunately. "Yes, so it appears."

"Sir, what do you recommend I do? What are the possibilities to my plight?"

I raise an eyebrow to the word plight and lean to see if he is holding a piece of paper, a script in front of him.

Like always, it only seems to dawn on them late in the term that they are failing the course, but never mind because if we put our collective heads together, we can find solutions, you and me, work things out, *sah*? Never too late—if we work together. Where there's a will there's a way?

I watch him fidget, glance out the window, mumbling some-thing about my scenic view of the Gulf and then back to fidgeting. "I'm not sure I can help you. What did you have in mind?"

He smiles at this, as if we have finally made some progress, a first step.

To be rude and angry and call him irresponsible and so on is no longer an answer, an option. I want him to admit fault, irresponsibility, immaturity. I want a testimonial, a confessional and only then will I tell him, "I can't help. Good luck."

A container ship is making its way from right to left. And for reasons that make no sense at all, there seems to be a relationship, a symbolism between the ship and this man-child fidgeting in front of me. A mysterious fit—moving from right to left.

"See that cargo ship?" I motion.

"Yes."

We turn to look as one. He waits for more, and so do I. Until finally, "Sorry. . . sorry, What is your name?"

"Abdullah. My name is Abdullah… and I am a senior and I need to graduate. But I need you. Your advice, your help. . ."

"I can't help you. I don't see how."

His fidgeting done because now it has become serious, he says, "Perhaps there will be a way tomorrow."

I like this comment and respond with, "Yes, come by tomor-row. . ."

He likes this answer. "What time?"

I check my calendar, and yes, I have a meeting at ten. "Ten o'clock tomorrow will be fine."

"Ten o'clock tomorrow."

"*Nam.*"

"Thank you, sir. By the way, your Arabic is excellent." And he backs out of my office like I am royalty.

The next morning I fully expect the new Nepalese security guard to recognize me, to good morning me as I walk by, but he does not—will not—and with hand firmly on cellphone holster, asks, "I.D. please."

"But I showed it to you yesterday. This is day two—you know me."

"I think so," he answers. "But you know, one can never be too sure." And holds out his hand for my I.D.

I quietly hand it over.

"Professor Martin, is it?"

"It is."

"Very good. You may pass."

His nametag says he is Ken, and he waves me through. Ken's teeth are a small milky white that have nothing to do with adulthood.

ॐ ॐ ॐ

Final exams are over and the academic void is palpable; for the time being all student thinking is finished. Two emails are waiting for me, both from Mary Christo in Nigeria who would like to share her inheritance with me. The telephone does not ring. Taking advantage of the lull, I lock my door. By noon there have been two knocks with doorknob twisting. Samba music softly twirls down the hallway, and for the first time in what feels like a long time I smile.

The Filipina nurses are headed home extra loud and happy today. The one in front seems to be the joke-teller because whatever she says causes the others to laugh, one of them throwing her head back in a strange horsey way, which creates greater laughter. I find myself smiling at this happy troupe, as if in some way they are my idea.

Before I leave, two end-of-the-day emails tell me that the dean and president would like to meet with me—at my convenience. I quickly respond with "How about tomorrow at 8:00?" This, I know, will never do, and sure enough, "How about ten o'clock?"

This is no coincidence, and I wonder what is so important that calls for a two-email approach. I open the door to an empty hallway. I listen for footsteps. There are none. Walking out of the building is like walking into a big wet heat, it sucks at my shirt, a fog jumps to my sunglasses. The sweat is immediate, and I can only think that that is a physiological impossibility, that there has to be some kind of prelude to things like this—a pre-sweat warning?

By now a new Nepalese shift is at the gates. This guard is white-haired with bad teeth and has known me for years. As I pass, I say, "Good bye, Karl."

He answers with, "Dr. Martin, good luck," smiling, showing me all of his bad teeth. I stop and stare.

৵৵৵

On Saturday morning the Indians and Pakistanis, like always, are playing cricket in the now-empty parking lot. There is much yelling, even when there is nothing to yell about. I stop to watch. The waiting and standing around continues, as, apparently, the ball has been lost under some car, in the bushes, or maybe not. This calls for some general squatting in the parking lot, in the morning heat while somebody's son searches for the ball—one cricketer pointing his way, another that way. A circus of shouting.

Just as I take the corner, I am startled with a "*Salaam. Fee makhfar greeb?*

"*Salaam,* sorry, what?"

He blinks to my 'sorry, what' before realizing what he is dealing with, and now backing up a step or two, reconsidering, utters, "Police station, where?"

"Police station, where?" I parrot.

"*Nam,* yes."

That's when I point down the street, motioning to the right. "Go straight, then right," I say.

He watches my hand flutter right, and nods.

"Straight then right then look to the left. You'll see it there." And to help him I motion again.

All done watching my hand, he says, "Ok." He wants to shake my hand and I let him.

As I watch him walk the way of my pointing, I think about how I have given him terrible directions, and how he will be lucky to find anything like a police station if he does what I said. There is still time to stop him, call him back, maybe squat with him in the dust behind the bus stop and draw a map in the sand. "Go to the roundabout. See this is a roundabout, then go right, see 3 o'clock, see? Then, walk 200 maybe 300 meters, maybe a little more and then look left," drawing a square in the dust to show him what a police station to the left looks like. "See this?" In the end, I am sure we will shake hands again. Meanwhile, he continues to walk and I continue to watch him and say nothing, thinking he will ask somebody else. Come to think of it, at least I sent him in the right direction, and that's something.

I told them that I would only be on campus for an hour, and she said, "Fine," which of course almost always has nothing to do with fineness. The daughters were watching the TV, and when I said, "Be gone an hour, probably less," the older one—who, no thanks to me, only got an 82 on the math quiz—turns to "Shhhhh."

By the time I walk to campus my shirt is wet, my face a healthy glistening. Once in my office it is too cold and I half-seriously think about taking off my shirt but no, that will never do. Someone has managed to wedge a piece of folded blue paper under my door and I step on it when I come in. When I unfold it, there is only one word: YES. I look again. YES. It is written in a black inky scrawl. YES. Just as I consider slipping it into the garbage can, I change my mind and pin it to the cork board. *There.* When I think of who to tell I have received a yes note, only Marshall comes to mind. This is perplexing because YES and Marshall with dragons are not compatible. I sit, move papers around and walk to the copy machine. I copy my right hand, then my left. I listen for others but I am the only fifth-floor person on a Saturday.

When I return home, she announces that we need a vacation. The girls, who are still in front of the TV, turn as one to say yes. So she says it again. "We need a vacation." A vacation is not out of the question. In fact, I am surprised we haven't thought of it sooner. But, for the time being, it is simply a spurt of energy on her part, and she disappears into the other room; they watch her go, and then turn to offer me a fatherly glare of indifference before returning to their TV.

ʗʗʗ

"Are you busy, Professor?"

When I look up, I immediately think she is too young to be the stuff of college, so frail and thin-limbed. "Please come in."

"May I sit?"

"How may I help you?" I ask waiter-like.

"I am not a student here, you know. Not me."

I think about responding, but nothing comes.

"Yes well, they said I should speak to you. When I asked, they said you would know, as department chair. You could tell me."

I almost ask who the they are but, on second thought, it doesn't matter. "Well, they are right, I am the chair."

This makes her smile. "May I get to the point?"

"Please do."

"Someday I want to major in English, you know. When I finish high school, I want to come here if you'll have me and major in your English department, if that's alright."

"Completely. But they didn't send you here to ask me that, surely."

"No, not exactly," she says with something like a blush, "but they want me to do something else; they think computer science or engineering is a good idea, a better idea, even accounting would be nice."

"All admirable professions, and can I assume that the they are Mom and Dad? Assorted cousins? The they?"

"Even Grandma and Uncle Hamad. My older brother thinks English is a bad future. How did you know?"

"Ah," holding up both hands as if I am getting ready to do magic "you forget, I am the chair."

At this point she should be smiling, maybe even a giggle, but no, just wide-eyed frailty.

"And," dropping my magic hands, "you would like for me to convince you, Mom and Dad, maybe even Uncle Hamad that the English major is in fact a noble major, worthy of righteous acclaim, although I must confess that in comparison to those other disciplines you mention, the world of the English major can be—how can I say—a financially-challenging endeavor. This, I imagine, Mom and Dad have said as much."

"Professor chairman, I don't really know about all of that but I do know that I like to read. That must count for something, don't you think? I like to read stories, and I want to do something like that when I grow up, read stories. Can I get paid for reading books? Isn't that what it's all about?"

The telephone rings and I let it.

"Shouldn't you answer that?"

"No, you keep forgetting I am the chair."

"Sorry."

"Yes, I like that: getting paid for reading books. I never thought of it that way, but, in essence, you're not wrong."

The smile returns. "Still, what am I to do? They want this, I want that. Please tell me."

For the first time her face suddenly loses its soft teenness as a frown ripples across her forehead, waiting for me.

"Chairman?"

"Yes?"

"Please tell me that if I major in English," surveying my office, at my full bookcases, the tiny towers of files and papers stacked on the floor, the big brightness of the Gulf from five floors up… "that it is the right thing. No matter what they say, even insist on, that this English major is the right decision."

"And when you grow up and have your college degree, what then? What is it you want to do, or, as they say: What do you want to be?"

The blush returns and she looks down at her hands, and when she speaks, I can't hear her.

"Sorry, I didn't…"

"You, Professor. I want to be you."

This time when the telephone rings I quickly answer it.

�ි�ි�ි

When the air from the large corner fan hits his hair exactly right, it flops, right to left. And if it is an interesting topic: about him, his publications, the many critics who have praised his books, 'Did I ever tell you about my Harvard lectures, how about the two at Stanford?' the important people he has met, known—the many photos cluttering his desk to prove it—he pays no attention to the flipflopping of his hair. But I do, and as he goes on about the time he had a man-to-man talk with the Amir, I nod at the right times while secretly watching his hair. Eventually he moves on to why he called the meeting. "A nasty business this higher education: so many bruised egos to contend with. Students claiming they've been wronged, treated unfairly, disrespected, is it. Not to mention the grown-ups, the professors: treated unfairly, disrespected in return."

Nodding to all of this, waiting for some sliver of clarity.

As he pats his flipflopping hair flat, I eye the dean and she is busy poking at her telephone, the wisp of a smirk.

"Martin, it's your department."

"It is?"

"Yes, your department. You know, we've had complaints."

"We have?"

"More than one, a bunch in fact. Batches of emails, telephone calls, even a meeting or two; some sort of unhappiness there, and they are blaming you, as chair."

"They are?"

"Yes, Ros and I, from your colleagues." He reaches across his desk to pick up a very white sheet of paper. In fact, I don't remember ever seeing a piece of paper so white. "They say you are not doing your job, not supporting them, not, . . ." looking harder into the white page, "not doing what is expected of a credible chair." That's the word they're using: "credible", waving the paper at me.

Ros is suspiciously quiet, looking out the window, now down at her ankles, window, ankles.

"Don't suppose my colleagues offer any details, any specifics? My colleagues."

The president stares at the paper. "No, but there is something here about details available upon request. That's what it says, what they say." More waving of the paper. As the three of us wait, his phone rings and he lets it.

"Well, as you know I've done my best, done my all, as they say." Thinking that this was enough, but both wait, and so, "Can't please everybody, right?"

He nods, she doesn't.

"Well, what's to be done?" he asks.

"Quell the revolt, I suppose. Or a new chair would do the trick. a new face to run things?"

"It's a thought," he says.

She returns to her telephone, her ankles, with more smirking.

He lets the phone ring.

"Is there anything else?" I ask.

She says, "Should there be? Isn't that enough?"

When I get up to leave, they remain seated.

"Meet with your colleagues, talk to them," he says.

"I do. I have. We do it every month, like clockwork."

Reaching over to float the white paper onto his desk. "One last-end-of-the semester meeting. You know, to clear the air before they disappear into the summer. Give them a pep talk. We all like pep talks."

When the phone rings again he answers it. The meeting is over.

ৰ্ণৰ্ণৰ্ণ

There is something like a carnival going on outside, on the soccer field. The music is loud, with much shouting into a microphone. If I place my head flat against the bookcase and turn just right, I can see the tip of a crowd; some students are clapping, most not. I strain to recognize the music but of course cannot. More clapping followed by bits and pieces of cheering. More microphone talk, followed by laughter, then booing, back to laughter. I turn to look at my cork board: YES.

Sara is in a strangely good mood, and I watch her as she talks with two students in mid-hallway. She is smiling, her hands full of flitty tossing and turning. Moments later she is at my door, leftovers of a smile on her lips, her hands twitching at her waist. "And happy end of term to you, Herr Chair."

"Likewise. That exciting, is it?"

Shrugging, but refusing to give up her smile. "It has its moments. Besides. . ." her hands at her sides, ". . . besides, there is news, you know."

"News?"

She moves closer, leaning over the desk. "I might be leaving, but it's a secret." Finger to her lips. "I might be leaving. Isn't that news? Good news?"

This has all the markings of a dangerous question. But I have not been department chair all these years for nothing, and reply, "If that's what you want."

She smiles, showing me all her teeth. "Yes, exactly."

For just the smallest moment I consider two things: my YES, and I wonder if she is drunk. I look down at my dusty shoes—*I need new shoes*—and when I look up, she is gone.

I steel myself for others, more to come.

More music, more microphone talk that, I believe, is some kind of Arabic rap. So yes, there will be others, I am sure of it.

Fittingly, the call to prayer fills the air: *La-ilaha-illa-Allah. There is no god but the God.*

11

The call for an urgent meeting comes from Thomas. He writes that it won't take long, but things must be decided, made clear, that, "As we all know, change can be a very positive thing, and I (we) would like to broach this subject at the meeting, as sensitive as it may be for some."

I immediately delete the message. That is when I look to my corkboard YES, and ... and it is gone. I search the floor, peek through files and books. I look again. It is gone. I step into the hallway to seek out the cleaning woman who goes by the name of Kunsun or Kanson or maybe Koomsoon. She is an ancient Sri Lankan whose shoes have always been too large and bulky, who spends more time on the stairwell talking on her telephone than doing anything that resembles cleaning. And sure enough, I find her on the stairwell, telephone in hand, shoes off, rubbing her foot.

"Where did you put my YES?" I demand.

"Yes?"

"Yes, my YES, what have you done with it?"

"Yes?"

"Yes, did you throw it away? Why did you do that? My YES. Anybody could see it was not garbage, not waste. Why would you do that?"

"*Shinu?*"

A neat package this one: rubbing a wizen foot with one hand, looking up at me with telephone in the other, all wrapped in a wide toothless grin.

I wait. She grins.

When I say, "Never mind" and walk away, leaving her to her stairwell, she answers, "Ok. Have a nice day."

࿓࿓࿓

Before heading home I have orders to pick up bread, eggs, carrots and three potatoes 'but make certain they are firm and hard, if they aren't hard, they're no good—double check.' Having done my duty and double checked for firmness, I slip in behind a man with young daughter at the checkout line.

"And I want this one and some of that one, and even this little blue one, . . so cute, don't you think? Oh, Daddy, look at this, the red one with stars, and at. . . Daddy, you aren't looking?" she continues, her tiny finger pointing at each and every chocolate candy bar on the shelf.

He frowns down at her, grabs her by the arm and leaning into her face says, "We talked about this. No candy. I warned you before coming in. Didn't I? Didn't I? I warned you." All done, he lets her arm drop.

Silent now, she stares down at her dirty white shoes, her

lips pressed tight, wringing her hands until they are a blotchy red and white. Meanwhile, I wait patiently behind them, holding tomorrow's breakfast and lunch in hand, looking off into the depths of the supermarket—into the aisle of breads and cheeses and cookies—to show them I haven't seen, I haven't heard.

The sign reads Express Lane: 10 items or less. It is very clear, spelled out in bright red letters, the number 10 underlined. He has more than 10 items, anybody can see that, his green hand basket overflowing. I have eight items, nine if you count chewing gum. As he begins to unload his basket, lining up one at a time, single file his more than 10 items across the countertop, I wait for the cashier to notice, to point to the sign, to say... But no, and the best she can do is chirp, "Good afternoon, sir."

Because the row upon row of candy looms impossibly close, at her shoulder, exactly at mouth level, she can't help but glance one more time, a neat line of brightly wrapped red and blue candy bars, and, on tiptoes, she has no choice but to say again, only louder, bigger, "Daddy, look, look. I want this one and that blue one, and..."

When he slaps her across the top of her head, she stumbles, righting herself just in time before almost falling into a rack of potato chips. With that same slapping hand, he takes hold of her neck, and bending down, his teeth up against the soft whorl of her ear, hisses, "I warned you."

She cries the silent cry of a five-year-old who is surrounded by strangers at a supermarket, her face growing wet and red. This time when I look away, I'm looking to see if I am the only one who has seen; if I am the only witness to what has just happened. Is it possible? When I look to see, turning this way and that, there are only shoppers shopping; people driving their grocery carts, swerving to avoid collisions.

With his one hand still strongly clamped around her neck, his other hand digs deep into his pocket, probing for money. Her face wetter, redder, she stares into the smooth tiled floor, as if a tiled supermarket floor has suddenly become so special. That's when it happens: because when his hand climbs out of his pocket fat with money, a five-dinar bill flutters gently to the floor. By the time it finishes stretching, uncurling, pushed this way and that by the tiniest of supermarket breezes, it has found its way to the tip of my shoe. She sees it the same time I do. Together we stare at the money. Her face grows quiet and even something like serious as she turns to tug at his sleeve, whispering, "Daddy? Daddy?" But Daddy, all done paying, gives her arm a furious tug, and just like some well-designed spring box, her mouth flies open, her eyes squint shut. As he chats with the cashier about the weather, how, 'Oh, yes, it is most definitely getting warmer, and, yes, Ramadan is just around the corner, it won't be long now,' laughter all around, that's when I slowly place my shoe on top of the five dinar. She gapes up at me, as if she can't believe. I press a finger to my lips.

All done shopping with his daughter, he politely thanks the cashier, saying, "See you again and have a nice day," and she, being a cashier, replies, "Yes, I will, and come again," and together, yanking her away by the arm, she stumbling to keep up, father and daughter move toward the exit, leaving me to be next. Almost at the exit now, the sunlight streaming yellow across the tile floor, and as I watch them leave, for the smallest moment she is able to twist away from his grasp, and craning her head to look back she waves good bye.

"Good afternoon, sir," the cashier chimes. "And how are you today?"

I answer with a smile, "Fine. I'm just fine."

Stepping out of the store with my plastic bag, I am surprised to see that a gang of dark purple bruised clouds have drifted in from the north, and just like Malaysia revisited, a downpour, along with a jagged display of thunder and lightning fills the air. I think about walking through it but it is overwhelming and I lean into somebody's doorway to wait it out. I watch others walk happily soaked as if it is nothing, every now and again, stopping to shake themselves doggy like. It isn't long before the storm has done its duty and tumbles on. The streets and sidewalks sparkle, all of which makes me think I am in another country.

When I get home, except for the dog that is happy to see me, that is happy to see anyone, it is silent. I feed him to make him even happier. All three of them arrive at once, laughing about something they saw, and when I ask what it is they, as if rehearsed, answer, "Nothing." Apparently, this is funny too. But never mind, because for the rest of the day and even part of the next I feel as if I have won something, and even Marshall's "Hail Caesar, Nero, is it?" ricochets off into the moonscape ceiling.

I watch a handful of students in graduation garb heading toward the auditorium, a crowd of sisters, brothers, cousins with hobbling grandmas not far behind. The grandpas stroll ahead of their wives, smoking their cigarettes, flicking ash as they go; every now and again, slowing, to let their wives catch up, taking photographs, holding balloons, carrying two, no three boxes of what can only be cakes.

When I arrive at Reedah's office, she is on the telephone and eyes me like an irritant. "What?"

"When is graduation?"

"Today of course, at 2:00. Everybody knows this."

"But there were no announcements, no emails. Nothing."

She motions for me to approach her computer, but not too close, and shows me the list of emails that, over the last two months, have periodically announced graduation, time, date. "All staff are encouraged to attend." When I lean closer, she says, "Don't touch the screen."

"How did I miss this? Six announcements. Six. How?"

"Normal."

"Sorry?"

"For you, it's normal."

Before I can consider how to take this, she is back on the telephone, shooing me away.

Of course she is wrong: this isn't me at all. Is it? *Six emails?*

The next morning I stop at a cafe that I have never gone to. I have walked by it hundreds of times; it's on the way, but there was nothing enticing about it: ancient dusty brickwork with three or four tables and chairs out front that are always empty, the wind having wrapped plastic bags and papers around the table legs. When I order toast and coffee, they bring me a slice of white bread and watery tea. I ask them to burn the slice of bread and say the word coffee again. This is understood. When I ask for some butter, just a little, holding up thumb and forefinger to show him a little, he nods and brings back a tissue with fork. He has replaced the tea with something darker. He waits for me to take a sip and I do and he smiles, saying, "Mexico." He waits for me to take another sip and I do and yes, as a matter of fact, it does taste like Mexico. This second sip sends him back to the kitchen. But that's not all because two tables behind me, I hear, "I love you."

Turning to look, the one being loved leans back in his chair, with cigarette and nods.

She says it again, "*Wallah, wallah*, I love you."

Again, nodding, followed by a bigger, longer puff on his cigarette, followed by a glance at his cellphone to see who might be calling, or not.

Their love-talk all done, she, too, can now turn to her cellphone.

ৰ৺ৰ৺ৰ৺

The newspaper tells me, yet again, that death and dying continue to be routine across the Middle East. I have grown weary of this mindless killing, this daily tally of who was in the wrong place at the wrong time. This idea of people hating others so much that the only solution is to end their lives has become hopelessly overwhelming, and often the best I can do is quickly turn to the sports page, or maybe read about which movie star has fallen in or out of love today.

Huddled near the elevator are three *dishdashas*, talking amazingly fast, something like a chatter. The elevator opens, they enter and when I follow all chatter stops. Two of us watch the floor numbers light up as we descend, the others look down at their shoes, at the scuffed elevator floor. I wonder what is so silent and secretive even in Arabic that they dare not say a word. Just before we arrive at the ground floor, I turn to the one who hasn't stopped watching his feet for five floors. "How are things?" He is genuinely taken by surprise and answers like some cartoon character, "Who me?" The other two turn to look at him; their stares say stop. When the elevator door yawns open, they insist I leave first. Once free of the elevator they restart their chatter. Before the elevator door shuts, I look back to see if there might have been another, someone I hadn't noticed—some administrator, counsellor, someone who commands silence.

I walk to the Diner and sit at a four-chaired table as if I am expecting others. Before I can even decide if I am hungry, if I even want to be there, Charles with bulbous chef hat, steps out of the back room and places a cup of coffee in front of me. His hands are large—two of my thumbnails would fit handily into his one—and even though I see him coming out of the corner of my eye, I spy nothing like a white coffee cup.

"Here you go. On the house."

"Ah, hello, nice of you. What's the occasion?"

Holding his chef hat straight with one hand, wiping the other on his apron, he shrugs, "No special reason. I can give away coffee if I want to."

Right then the three chattering *dishdashas* make their way into the diner, and upon seeing me wave like we are friends. They sit on the other side of the diner, under the Marlon Brando with motorcycle photograph.

"Good semester, Dr. Martin? Did your duty, did you?"

"As a matter of fact, I did, Charles, I sure did."

He smiles a smile that is missing one important front tooth, and before I can stop myself, ask, "Charles, what happened to your tooth?"

"Ah," waving aside my question with his large coffee-cup fist, "Ah, that was a long time ago. Young and silly, a long time ago."

Nodding because I know what he means.

"Ok, well back to work, Doc. Good to see you." And he disappears back through the swinging doors.

When I take a sip of his on-the-house coffee it is cold. I try it again, thinking this can't be right. The second sip is colder. I can't decide if this is the stuff of anger or not. *An honest mistake? Has to be.* I think about drinking it anyway, as a kind of protest against. . . against what?

The three *dishdashas* are arguing over what looks to be a textbook. They take turns saying, "*Lah, lah, lah.*" Finally, one of them slams the book shut and the other two look at him to see if he is serious, and he is, then isn't, then is again. They stop to look at the wall, at Marlin Brando and his motorcycle.

Fingering the cold but free coffee when I look down, there is a coin, 100 *fils*. I nudge it with my shoe, and look to see who might be watching, and there is only the three *dishdashas* watching Marlin. Again, I poke it with my shoe. It is only 100 *fils*, and I wonder if I should even bother. Just as I decide that I should, the backroom doors swish open and Charles re-emerges. He comes directly to me, bends down, and pockets the 100 *fils*, saying, "Sorry, I forgot my money." He grins.

For the rest of the day, I will consider this.

༚༚༚

Daughter and Father are at my door, and I stand up to meet them. He smiles and holds out a hand to shake while she, with daughterly indifference, watches our hands grasp.

"Please," and I motion for them to enter but he insists I return to my desk first. Their tale is one of a professor's rudeness towards her, his only daughter; never mind the grade, it's all about being harsh and insensitive and how he even smirked when she confided in him, how she was interested in medicine, and someday, *inshallah*, hoped to become a doctor, *inshallah*, like her mother and two uncles. But he only smirked, this Professor, maybe even a snort and she immediately turned and left the classroom. "So yes, forget the grade, that is nothing. But the snorting and smirking at medicine, that is uncalled for, Professor."

I concur that it does not seem right, and when I ask what it is they would like for me to do, he, his smile all gone now, says, "A reprimand, of course. Something in writing, something for his file. You have personnel files?"

She with green fingernails, balled softly in her lap, nods to this. "Yes absolutely, something must be done. I agree. No worries, I will bring him to task, you have my word."

"Well," getting up, "that's good enough for me. Farah, you hear that, his word and so we are done here. Let's go tell your mother."

Once they are gone and I shut the door, it dawns on me that they never mentioned the culprit. But never mind, because even though I can guess who the he is, I send out a soft reproof to all in the department to refrain from smirking and snickering, or even snorting at any students who might express an interest in, someday, attending medical school. "Anyone caught smirking will have an official reprimand placed in their file. Thank you."

Peter responds, "Noted."

Sara says, "Shouldn't it read 'his/her'?" And so on.

৵৵৵

At home I turn on the TV and steadily click from channel to channel to channel, although I do stop to watch a golfer grimace when he misses a short four-foot putt. Finally, I turn it off and see the dog at the screen door, staring in. I ask him what he wants, and he answers with a doggy moan and frantic tail wagging. I ask him if he has anything else to say. "Is that it? Anything you want to tell me? Have a complaint maybe? Don't like my teaching methods? My grading does not meet your needs? How about my attitude? Am I disrespectful, maybe impolite? Anything at all?"

Front feet on the screen door, begging to be let in so he can speak with me closer—dog to man. Barking now. Until finally I say, "No." He turns, his tail-wagging all done for the time being, and moves off into the almost-garden.

It is the middle of the day and I shouldn't be home. But I did tape a note to my office door saying no office hours today. Because I almost never do things like this—a kind of chair hooky—my guilt is lukewarm. I take off my shoes and put my feet on the coffee table, on top of the fat western art book that nobody has opened for years. *Where'd that come from?* I hear the swish of midday traffic thataway, what sounds like children screeching from somewhere across the street. Jaffar's coughing laugh, like fingernails on a chalkboard. The dog is back at the screen door, thinking, I really didn't mean my No and he only wants to say he's glad to see me in the middle of the day and it's hotter than hell out here, and oh, by the way, would you mind giving me a little extra water, and come to think about it, some of those doggy bits sound pretty good too. So yes, so very happy to see you.

I get up and walk upstairs.

I turn on the fan then think about shutting the door but then remember it is just me and the dog. The telephone rings, and it is Reedah wondering where I am.

"Home. I am home."

"Are you sick?"

"No, nothing like that. Why? Some meeting I forgot? Some urgent dean conference that can't wait? What? There's a note on my door, you know."

Reedah, who is very good at being quiet when she has to be, is now. When I step to the window, the dog has moved into the weeds and is looking up at me, as if he knew that's exactly what I would do. There is something all wrong with a dog knowing things like that.

"Sorry, Reedah. Is there something I can help you with, anything at all?"

"No, no, nothing like that. It is just, just that you're always here and now, for some reason, you are not. This is not the Dr. Martin I know, that's all. Nothing, really."

I wave to the dog and it barks, and for some silly reason this brings tears to my eyes: look what I can do, wave at my dog and it barks. "Good-bye, Reedah, I will be in tomorrow. See you then, tomorrow."

"Yes, I understand, but one last thing."

"Yes?"

"One final thing."

"Yes?"

"Just take care of yourself, Doctor."

I put the telephone down on the desk and wave again at the dog and again it barks and again there are tears.

First thing the next day, firmly situated in my office, at my desk, Reedah calls. "Feeling better?"

"Reedah, I wasn't feeling bad, was I? I mean, I wasn't sick."

"So you are feeling better?"

This, I determine, could turn into a lengthy conversation and so, for the sake of brevity, answer, "Yes."

The next day I take a new and longer way home just to see what the side-streets are all about. When I walk in, the place is full of blue and white balloons, which can only mean a birthday party is near. I take a seat next to a bundle of the blue balloons and when I do, she hurries over, asking, "Are you here for the party?"

'No, I am not. I just want to eat. Whose birthday is it?"

"Sorry, you can't sit here, this is for the birthday party people."

I look at the other tables, chairs, they are all ballooned blue and white. "Where can I sit?"

Together we look at the restaurant until someone from the backroom shouts, "Annie?"

"Where can a non-birthday party person sit?"

"Annie?"

"Stay," she commands, as she does two things: first, firmly places a hand on my shoulder, keeping me in the chair; second, and just as firmly, snatches the batch of blue balloons from the table and moves them to another table that is now doubly thick with blue balloons. "There," she says. "All is well, right?"

"Annie, where are you?"

"Maybe I should come back another time, a time when there is no birthday."

"Don't be silly."

She scurries to the backroom and I listen to what starts off as a muffled argument but quickly grows to unmuffled. When she returns, her cheeks are a new red. "I am so sorry, we can't serve you today with this party." She goes to the doubly crowded blue balloon table and brings the balloons back to my table.

"Whose birthday did you say it was?"

"Annie?"

As she walks me to the front door, she says sorry two more times, and I answer both times with an 'It's ok.' Once I am out on the sidewalk again, she locks the door, all the while her redness growing bigger, redder.

A couple of days later I try the restaurant again, but this time before I walk in, I peek to see if there is anything like balloons on tables, anything that hints of pending party. It is not the same waitress who welcomes me, and when I ask where she is, the other one, Annie, the girl says, "Oh, she left, you know. Don't know the details, but she left. Happens all the time, you know. People coming and going. Now, what did you want to order?"

I order a chicken sandwich and she slowly writes what I say, 'chicken sandwich', on a paper pad. She brings the sandwich on a blue plate and there is nothing wrong with it except the lettuce is leafy, limp and rusty around the edges. I eat it and pay and walk back out into the bright heat. All of this happens very quickly, which, strangely, feels nothing like eating at a restaurant. I had hoped for something else, something more, like the last time but come to think of it I don't even know what that means. Still, that's the problem, always has been: this middle-of-the-day mediocrity. More people like Annie would be nice.

As luck would have it—or not—days later I see ex-waitress Annie walking across the street across from the university, and I hurry to intercept her. "Hi."

She eyes me, frowning a "Hello."

"Don't remember me? At the restaurant the other day, birthday party, balloons, I couldn't stay."

She nods to this and then cocks her head as if she wants to see who might be behind me, following. "I don't work there anymore."

"I know, I know. But remember me?" I doggedly continue.

"Sorry, I don't, now if you'll excuse me." And she leaves me there on the sidewalk, in the middle of the day, with the heat blaring down.

"Annie?" I whisper, and she hears, turning to look at me one last time before shaking her head and walking faster.

12

Just when I think the jungle dreams are finished, all used up, I have another: of Africa, of a village in Africa. At first it is a quiet village: lazy white tails of breakfast smoke winding into the morning, a dusty grove to the right, the savannah to the left, lines of misty brown hill are everywhere. But then there comes a noise, a hum, like machinery approaching. And like a kind of magic the villagers suddenly appear, scurrying from their huts, shading their eyes to look eastward. There is chatter and the children bounce with joy. My dream-eye turns eastward too but sees nothing except a gray smoke. The humming grows louder, bigger. Looking harder now, the dream-eye sees that it is no ordinary gray smoke but something more, alive, a swarm of locusts. The humming turns to a clatter. It is then that the villagers, as one, turn their backs to the approaching swarm, extend their arms Christ-like and shut their eyes. With a swoosh, the locusts engulf them. The children giggle and squirm. A woman screams. The locusts are so thick and gray that the village flickers shut, disappearing. In the end, the swarm moves on, leaving the villagers bleeding, bruised and happy. The dream-eye moves in to investigate, and yes, they are smiling, touching their ears and noses and smiling. Although they speak Swahili, the dream tells me they are happy because they can hear and smell better. Swarming locusts are like that: helping themselves to everything in their path, even earwax and mucus.

I wake to a square of sunlight, heavy and hot across the bed. Like always I pull back the curtain to inspect the day; I look for clouds, the chance of rain, wind in the trees. But I am thinking of another time, another country. I do twenty push-ups and thirty sit-ups, sometimes thirty push-ups and twenty sit-ups. Either way it adds up to fifty. I don't like this exercise business, not if I can help it, but once finished I almost always think the same thing: *That'll show them.*

As I step into the bathroom, fronting the mirror cowboylike, something's not right but I'm not sure what until I edge closer, squinting; and sure enough there's a sliver of old skin hanging from the corner of my mouth. *It could have stayed there for hours, all day, and nobody would have said a word. Nothing like an 'Excuse me but you've got something white right there. Yeah, right there—something all white and dangly.'* Frowning extra hard until my eyebrows beetle. *That's what it's come down to: people happy to sit and stare and let a man go through life with bits of dead skin hanging from his face. Not right. Got to help a fellow out.* I ready my fingers to pull off the skin, to steady myself for the tiniest flicker of pain that is to follow, but it takes no pulling, and falls neatly onto a fingertip. I flick it into the sink, washing it down the drain. Turning my head this way and that, knowing all along there's only so much a man can do. Wondering how a beard would look, *Salt and pepper, more salt than pepper. Grow beards to hide something—warts, moles, funny lips.* There's a small, unimportant tapping at the door.

"I'm here."

Then, she pulls up a stool to watch me shave, watching in the mirror. After the first ski-like cheek stroke, she clears her throat and points out that, "In case you haven't noticed your teeth are yellow and mine aren't. In case you haven't noticed." I laugh at this, but once my shaving is almost done and she has jumped off the stool to get ready for school, I turn on the brightest light in the bathroom and snarl into the mirror. And of course she is right. Later, I will go to the store and buy one of those expensive teeth whiteners. If anybody asks, I will say it's for someone else, anyone else. Once home I will slip it into my pocket—just in case—walking quickly to the bathroom and hide it in the bottom drawer, a drawer full of hot water bottles and pale plastic tubing. For a week, maybe two, I will use it every morning; and just when I think there is something going on, a hint of that old whiteness returning, she will look up from her oatmeal, stare at me, take another bite and then making one of her ugliest faces, press a surprisingly hard finger to my lips, saying, "Still yellow. Monster yellow."

Back at the mirror, I look at my hair. More than ever it is important that it look right, that it lay right; and just when I think I've got it, my hands hovering at the ready, staring good and long, I remember the mirror's way is not the real way, and so I recomb, slanting everything the other direction. It looks all wrong, but I let the warm water run over my hands. This is the best part of the morning.

By the time I get downstairs, they are all gone: work, school, school. She left the newspaper for me. The front page is all about earthquakes in India, children shooting children, politicians, buses plunging hundreds of feet down cliffs in Mexico… The coal mines in China are killing their miners, weekly. I pour myself a cup of coffee, but before sipping I can't help but remember my teeth, and snarl.

⇛⇛⇛

Come to think of it I haven't seen Jaffar for days. Jacob is out front, on his stool, watching the cars take the speed bump too fast, scraping their undersides, shooting sparks. My car remains dusty and unwashed, the flowers un-watered, the hose nothing more than a green walkway squiggle. I walk up to Jacob and ask, "Where is Jaffar? I haven't seen him for a while."

Jacob, grimacing when a black Mercedes screeches over the speed bump, says, "Don't know. Haven't seen him."

I wait for more, but he continues to watch the speed bump with cars. And so, "No idea?"

He turns to look at me, trying out a grin that does not work. "Dr. Martin, I think Jaffar is gone. Maybe back to Egypt, but gone. So sorry."

"But why?"

Jacob takes his feet off the stool and fishes in his shirt pocket for a cigarette. But once he finds one, he changes his mind and puts it back. "Not sure, Dr. Martin, not sure. Something about being here is no longer a good idea. That's what he said. Things are changing here, you know," extending a hand towards the street. "I see it too but maybe he sees something bigger and more than me, *sah*? So, I think he decided to go, even escape, see what I mean? This place is no good for him anymore."

❧❧❧

For the first time since I can remember everyone is at the conference table before I arrive, even Ahmad, and surprisingly without his usual stack of student papers to grade. Marshall is wearing one of his sleeveless t-shirts, his dragons lazing on both arms. John and Peter are sitting next to one another, and for the first time I see a resemblance: their noses too long for their faces, wisps of hair that defy combing, that flutter and twitch even when there is no breeze. Sara is leaning off her chair, which means she would rather be somewhere, anywhere, else. At the end of the table is Thomas, who, I must admit, looks properly placed. Even Reedah finds the time to stick her head in to see what is what, giving me a look that is filled with sorrow, if not sorrow then a look asking, 'And what did you expect?' There is not much in the way of hellos as I sit facing Thomas at the other end of the table. It is then, the chair scraping and throat clearing all finished, that he begins with, "Well…" only to be interrupted by the wail of the fire alarm. Sara is the first one out of her chair, moving swiftly, determinedly toward the door; the others groan, waiting to see what others will do. Reedah's head appears for a second time, but this time with a different look, announcing, "No drill this. No drill. Everybody out." All of us except Marshall aim for the door.

"Don't believe it," he says. "Don't believe any of it." Arms behind his head.

"Marshall, you heard Reedah, let's go. You never know. Come on. You never know."

Locking his fingers firmly behind his head. "Don't be stupid but go ahead. I'll be here waiting when you return. Go on. Be gone."

In the hallway the wailing grows to a shriek, and I hurry, hands over ears. When I look to see who is with me, beside me, I am alone. I hear voices, the slamming of doors. "Don't take the elevator, you fool." I think about rushing to my office to…to… to do what? *Maybe I should turn around and retrieve Marshall? Retrieve? Fetch? It's the least I can do.*

It is true that when the fire alarm blares, it almost always means a drill, a test, to practice until we get it right. Regardless, the faded notice on the bulletin board insists we quickly leave the building, lock doors, don't take the elevators, and "make your way safely into the parking lot." With the blaring echoing down the hallway, for some reason I stop to reread this last part—'into the parking lot'.

The Nepalese security are herding everyone in the right direction, saying something which I can only guess means "This way, hurry, this way." I see security guard Ken grinning, excitedly, as if this is the most fun he has had in weeks. Peter is suddenly at my side. "Ah, another one of those infernal drills, I suspect."

"Of course." But then as if two words can never be enough, I continue with, "Certainly is hot today."

Peter considers this and just when I think he hasn't heard, announces, "Better to reign in Hell than serve in Heaven."

Two police cars come to a screeching halt, one right behind the other. The same familiar-faced policeman I saw the other day at the in-front-of-the campus traffic stop hops out of the first car, stepping quickly into the hallway. He sees me, smiles, saying, "Hello, Professor Martin, so good to see you again."

As we get ready to shake hands...

Later, they will tell me that that's when the blast threw us into the wall, with Peter flying magically one direction, me and the policeman another; and in that small space of tumbling through the air, I remember wondering how Peter could do something like that at his age. I think I was impressed, even jealous.

13

"What did you do?" Reedah asked, her face hovering balloon-like above me.

"What?"

"Do. What did you do?"

Meanwhile, somebody is tugging at my arm, asking me, "And what is your good name, sir?"

"What?"

"Your name? What is your good name?"

There is shouting, like soccer-match shouting. Someone is crying.

Reedah, leans back, hands on hips.

"Are the Spanish adjuncts ok?" I ask.

Now it is her turn to say, "What?"

"Are they?"

"Sir, your good name."

That someone has not stopped pulling my arm, and by now Reedah's face has floated away, leaving me to look up at a broken ceiling, splintered wood next to a skeleton of gray piping. Water is gushing. More shouting and this time when the arm-puller asks, "Can you hear me?" I turn to look and it is Early, the security guard.

"Hello, Early."

"I thought it was you."

Somebody, somewhere is demanding an answer: "Whose idea was this?" That's when I remember Peter's aerobatics but when I turn to see where he is, Early angrily says, "Don't move." But too late because I see a wide smear of blood across the floor.

Within hours we were famous, worldwide news, and for days there is video showing billowing black smoke, fire licking from windows, people running, lumps of debris in the streets. Overnight reporters are everywhere, not to mention the caravan of news trucks with their big-eyed satellite dishes. This goes on for days, until, suddenly, one morning, the news people are gone because a bigger, more devastating violence has erupted across the border, and just like that we are no longer famous.

⊱⊰⊱⊰⊱⊰

They said it would take weeks for the soreness to disappear and even then, the torn muscles will echo for months, even years. The good news is the bruises are already almost gone.

It is my first day out in what seems like a very long time, and I shuffle old-man-like towards a table, gently lowering myself into the chair. It is too hot to be out but I don't care, and others feel the same way.

I watch as they find an empty table for four, he on one side, she on the other and almost immediately he does two things:

smokes a cigarette and looks long and hard into the machine he carries in his left hand; while she, too, takes out her handy machine from her purse and stares intently into it. Meanwhile, their maid, not to mention what looks to be something like a three-year-old son, are walking along the harbor's edge, looking down at the flash of tiny fish, the many pigeons on the walkway behind them. It isn't long before the boy loses interest in the fish and makes for the pigeons, and of course it is not the maid's duty to say no, as he scares pigeons into the palms.

I sip my coffee. I ordered a donut but it is only for show. I am not hungry.

Back to the young couple who have now ordered their food, and seeing that the maid with son is in shouting distance, the mother returns to her machine, even pushing a button or two, bringing the screen to life. When the maid and son return, I can hear him doing his best to tell Mom and Dad all about the birds and fish and sailboats, and Mother waits for him to finish before saying, "That's fine."

I delicately shift in my chair but the soreness follows. Another sip of coffee just to be doing something.

By now the maid tells the son it is time to eat and placing him on her lap she helps him plunge a straw into a cup of chocolate milk while cutting pieces of pancake to slowly deliver into his open mouth. In the meantime, the husband is hard at work watching his machine, and now laughing. When the wife's machine beeps, although she frowns, she answers anyway, "Hallo". By now the son catches sight of a large calico worming its way through tables and chairs, and forgetting all about his pancake, not to mention the chocolate milk, he squirms on her lap to see what the cat is all about. The best she can do is give his chocolatey mouth a mighty wipe before he twists free.

After a kind of breakfast, the maid with three-year-old son have now lost sight of the cat so return to the harbor, the fish, while the pigeons, remembering him, head to the tall grass. Back at the table, the young mother and father, their machines still firmly gripped in their hands, are talking, and part of their talk has to do with children, how they are thinking of having another child. I look down at my feet to show them I am not listening, or watching. Another half-hearted sip. It is time for another child, *sah?* It sounds like a talk they have had before, but only now, at the harbor on the weekend, do they both agree, nodding and smiling and letting their fingers touch before returning to their machines. As he lights another cigarette, she half-turns to the son and maid who are no longer there, asking, "And how was your pancake?"

The son and maid are back at the water's edge. She has a firm grip on his shirt as he leans though the harbor railing to scatter a tiny handful of pebbles over the water. Both maid and son think this funny.

They removed the bandages weeks ago, leaving behind a rugged gangster scar on my cheek that, they assured me, will grow almost invisible, eventually. More people arrive.

Because it is sticky and warm, they roll out one of the big fans to place near their table. And so there they are: three women, sunglasses neatly positioned atop *hijabs*, under the palms, enjoying the harbor, chatting, minding their own business, when suddenly, the three-some squeal and jump up, knocking over chairs and assorted coffee cups, ripping a hole in the quiet harbor morning. The three women scatter in three different directions. I want to jump up, too, but can't, the aching rippling across my shoulders. The three of them, now safely away from their table, slowly, come together, one, hand covering her mouth, another hands-on hips, the third squatting to get a better looksee at the table with over-turned chairs. When I look, ready for something terrible, all I see is one of those scrawny harbor cats sitting in a nonchalant catty way, looking hard at me as if to say *What?*

Later, my first day out almost over, the coffee cold, the soreness flaring, she doesn't just push the baby carriage but drives it. I can see her coming from a longways off, as she weaves around walkers and talkers, steering the carriage around a cluster of palms and potted plants. She is looking directly at me, if not at me then at the empty table next to me, her destination. As she navigates the carriage through the maze of chairs and tables, I can see an easier route, a less zig-zagging way, but never mind because she hasn't taken her eyes off the empty table, as if someone will grab it at any moment no matter how hard she tries. Her face grows red, redder as she does something like a bulldozing, scraping chairs and tables out of the way, and just when she thinks she is through the clog of tables and safely onto the harbor walkway, her buggy catches the edge of a table, and the man's coffee cup storms, a tiny brown coffee-wave rolling into his lap. He jumps up, glaring at her, and the best she can do is stop, reconsider and say, "What are you looking at?"

When she finally arrives, she parks one of the carriage wheels on my foot before she plops down in a chair. Because baby carriage wheels are not heavy, I think nothing of it and easily lift it off and when I do, she says 'Sorry' while looking down at her hands. That is when I see that the baby carriage is empty, baby-less, and when I look to see where her child can be, there is nothing. No toddler chasing pigeons, no maid gently herding a child, nothing like a father. Her carriage parked, she reaches in to arrange a dirty blue blanket, tucking it neatly in here and there, smoothing it flat. I heard what she said to the man and prepare myself for her unhappiness, but surprisingly she turns to me like she had called this meeting, and thanks for coming, wondering..."And how are you today?"

I have decided to tell her how I am today, that my shoulders continue to ache, the red rawness in my back having grown to a prickly pink and, oh, by the way, remember hearing about those explosions at the university... but before I can, she decides that, come to think of it, this empty table next to me is not for her, never has been, and, "It was so good talking to you," she and her baby carriage lurch away into the harbor sunlight.

14

By now Peter is off his crutches, content to hobble, and when I say, "A cane would be a good idea," he angrily counters with, "Who needs a cane?" But for some reason he is in no hurry to move on; in fact, he stops to look at me.

"What?"

He shrugs and hobbles away.

"You've got that meeting today, you know?" she says in her best statement-that-sounds-like-a-question way.

"I do?"

"You know you do," she growls.

I make my way pass the many workers who, seemingly, are more interested in laughing than working, and when I turn to see what's so funny, I see nothing more than the stuff of broken buildings. I continue, weaving my way around the many blue tarps that cannot cover it all, and here and there blistered, smoke-stained windows peek out. They have placed concrete barriers in the street, and a police car with flashing red and blue lights sits at the entrance. Sometimes a policeman will sit in the car and talk on his phone, but most of the time it is empty, just the flashing red and blue lights. None of the elevators work so I take the stairs. As I enter his office, I remember it being bigger. He is on the telephone and motions for me to take the one chair directly in front of his desk. Once he finishes, by way of a good morning he says, "Let's not beat around the bush. We've got a lot to do."

We?

I respond with a "Surely." I am still thinking of Peter's gaze.

Pigeons flutter down and begin their back and forth across his window ledge, The big cloud-less sky, a tired blue.

"We are in need of a dean, you know," he says like he is ordering food.

"We are?"

"You know we are."

"I do?"

There is a siren and we wait for it to finish. That's when I realize that he has yet to sit down.

"We're in need of a new dean, you know this." Running his fingers along his chin. "Her side of the building was annihilated, the whole side ripped away." He refuses to sit down.

"No, no, you can't be serious," I say.

"Which part?"

"The part you're not saying."

"Fraid so."

"But I'm the Chair."

"No longer." Folding his arms headmaster-tight across his chest. "We've a new Chair."

"We do?"

"It's been decided."

"But I'm the Chair."

"Sara has taken over. In fact, she was happy to volunteer her services. Almost giddy, I must say."

"Sara? Sara Crane?? That can't be right; there's been some mistake," I say in a desperation that surprises even me. "No, wait. The others. What do they say? The others?"

"Mullen and Chaplin think it's grand. Their word, 'grand'. The others, silence." Back to rubbing his chin, as if considering.

When I look down at my shoes, I see one of the shoelaces has worked its way loose, and as I lean over to tie it, in a mild panic, he says, "What are you doing?" Quickly, seeing what's what, he sighs. "We are in need of a dean."

My shoestring successfully retied, it is my turn for folded arms. A wave of laughter from the workers. The cooing of pigeons.

"We've met, we've discussed, we've decided; you're the new Dean. It's a done deal, congratulations."

"No wait. There's been a mistake."

"Congratulations. *Mabrouk.*"